Rachel

BOOKS BY
MARY CHRISTNER BORNTRAGER

Ellie
Rebecca
Rachel
Daniel

A SEQUEL TO *ELLIE* AND *REBECCA*

Rachel

Mary Christner Borntrager

HERALD PRESS
Scottdale, Pennsylvania
Waterloo, Ontario

Library of Congress Cataloging-in-Publication Data
Borntrager, Mary Christner, 1921-
   Rachel : a sequel to Ellie and Rebecca / Mary Christner
Borntrager.
     p.   cm.
   ISBN 0-8361-3539-3
   I. Title.
PS3552.07544R34   1990
813'.54—dc20   90-45033
                                                CIP

The paper used in this publication is recycled and meets the
minimum requirements of American National Standard for
Information Sciences—Permanence of Paper for Printed Library
Materials. ANSI Z39.48-1984.

Scripture quotations are from the King James Version of *The
Holy Bible.*

The baptismal questions and responses in chapter 24 are from
Donald B. Kraybill, *The Riddle of Amish Culture* (The Johns
Hopkins University Press, 1989), p. 100.

*To all loving
grandparents everywhere
and to my own dear
niece Rachel*

Contents

1
A Surprise Letter

Ellie watched David coming down the lane from the mailbox. She could tell right away that he was excited. He was walking with a jaunty step and whistling that happy little tune which told her that he was pleased.

"Ellie," he called out. "Ellie, we got a letter from James and Rebecca."

Their daughter Rebecca had left the Amish while keeping company with James, a Mennonite youth. Seven years ago, her minister husband, James, took Becky and their three small children to Central America in mission work.

"A letter!" exclaimed Ellie. *"Mach's uff* (open it)," she said, wringing her hands in delight.

The family now included four children. Baby Rachel was born soon after they left North America. David's hands trembled as he opened the envelope and scanned its contents.

"Well, what did they write?" asked his wife impatiently. "Are they all well?"

"Give me a little time to clean my specs, and I'll tell you what they wrote." David called his glasses "specs," and Ellie knew he was teasing again.

"*Ach* (oh), give me that letter. You are slower than molasses in January," she said, laughing. Ellie took the pages and began to read. "Oh, David," she exclaimed, "they're coming home! Just think, we haven't seen them for more than seven years and now—oh my!—they're coming home.

"I hope the children still remember us. Do you think they will? It has been so long. Why, Rachel won't know we are her *Dawdies* (grandparents). And we don't even know who she looks like."

"I imagine she looks like Rachel," said *Dawdy* (Grandpa).

Ellie and David had never seen a picture of her and didn't want to. They preferred face-to-face relationships. As good Amish people, they did not believe in having photos of themselves or others. They obeyed the Ten Commandments, in which God says, "Thou shalt not make unto thee any graven image or any likeness of any thing. . . ."

James and Rebecca respected her parents' faith and sent no pictures of their growing family. Anyhow, there were few to send. They both felt that what little money they had should be put to better use.

"They're coming back," Ellie repeated eagerly. She found it hard to believe.

David interrupted her: "Are you going to read

the rest of the letter, or just stand there saying, 'They're coming home'?"

"Ach," laughed Ellie, "I'm so *verhuddelt* (mixed up). Here, you read it. I'm going to cry." She did, too, but they were happy tears.

"*Mammi* (Grandma)," David said, "you cried when they left and now you are crying because they are coming home." But he knew they were tears of joy. Leading his wife to the rocker, he said, "Sit here and I'll read it all to you. Maybe they're just coming for a furlough. I wonder when they plan to get here."

Grandma blew her nose and settled back in her comfortable rocker as her husband began to read.

Dear Grandpa and Grandma,

We are coming back to the States. I had to write this first of all. The children are so excited, especially Rachel. She constantly asks questions about so many things. The older ones can hardly wait to see you and their cousins. Neither can James and I.

My letter can't be lengthy. All missionaries have been ordered to leave this country at once because of trouble here. I can't write about it, but as soon as everything is taken care of here, we will be on our way. This will probably be by the ninth of April, which gives us only a few days to get our things together. We may even be in the States before this letter reaches you.

We have written to Grandpa Millers, and they will meet us when we arrive. James felt we should stay, even in the face of danger, but after much prayer and careful consideration, we are leaving. We will miss the many friends we have made here and must now leave behind. Our hope is that we have given them something which can never be taken from them. Many have learned how to trust in God and be more self-reliant. Pray for our safety.

Love to you both, Rebecca.

"I won't sleep a wink until they get here safe and sound," Ellie declared. "It doesn't matter how grown-up our children are, I still feel I must mother them."

"That's always been evident," commented David. "To me, that's the mark of a good mother." Ellie was glad he felt that way.

There would be so much to do to get ready to welcome back her daughter and family. "Oh, I must clean the house right away. The windows need washing, and I want to make sure the bedding is all clean and fresh. Some of my blankets don't get used very often. Maybe we should hang them out to air this afternoon yet. That sun is out so bright. You will need to go to the store for some groceries, too. I'll want to do some baking."

"Now, Mammi, your floors are clean enough to eat off of, and the rest of the house is fine, too. We have been able to live in it. Besides, I'm sure James and Rebecca aren't going to pay attention to the looks of the house. It's us they want to see."

"I'm going right over and tell Roy's. They will be surprised, too," Ellie told David.

Roy and Lydia lived in the big farmhouse right beside the *Dawdy Haus* (the grandparents' small house). They had a large family, and Grandma remarked lovingly that you had to be careful not to step on any children. They often came running to greet her.

Today was no different. Little Scottie met her at the door. She never could understand why their son Roy and his wife chose such an English name for one of their children. He was a cheerful, obedient child, so she had decided she could accept that name. As he grew older he was Scott, and the Dawdies liked that better.

"Where is your *Mudder* (mother)?" Ellie asked.

"I think she went upstairs."

"Run up and tell her to come down. I have wonderful good news."

Scott just stood and looked at his Grandma. "Mammi, have you been crying?" he asked.

"*Mach schnell* (go quickly)," she answered. Without delay the boy ran upstairs, calling, "Mom, come right away. Grandma is here and wants to talk to you. I think she is crying." Lydia dropped her broom and rushed downstairs. She was alarmed.

"Mammi, what's wrong?" she asked.

"*Nix, nix ist letz* (nothing, nothing is wrong). No, everything is all right. Becky is coming home."

"Just Becky?" Lydia asked.

"No, the whole family. We had a letter today. She thought they would be leaving by the ninth of April. That means they could come any time now."

"Are they coming for a long visit?" asked Lydia.

"They are coming to stay. Just think, we have never seen Rachel. I wonder what she is like. But now I must hurry back and get busy." Several of the children were catching their grandma's excitement and gathered around her.

As Ellie opened the door to her little house, she began to cry again.

"How are you going to get anything done if you have to wipe tears all the time?" asked David.

"Well, what's that I see on your own face?" she asked, as she saw him dab at some trickles.

"Ach," he responded, *"yuscht Wasser Drobbe* (oh, just drops of water)."

2
Meet Rachel

Although at first she was excited, it seemed to be harder for Rachel to leave for North America than for any of her siblings. This, however, was no surprise to her family. Her sister, Susie, and brother Timothy remembered friends and family from earlier times, as did their brother Mark, though only faintly. Mark was only four when they left for Central America.

"Can we take my friend Nedra, too?" asked Rachel.

"No, I'm afraid we can't," her mother told her.

"Well, then I'm not going," she decided.

"Would you want to stay here, Rachel, and all the rest of us go without you?" her sister Susie asked.

"No, but I don't want any of us to live in the States. I want us all to stay here. Nedra and I have fun together, and when she doesn't have much to eat, I like to share with her. Who will do that if we go away? Why do we have to leave, anyway?" she complained tearfully.

James was helping pack what little they were taking with them. He heard Rachel lament the fact that they were moving. "Come here, Rachel," her father called. "None of us thought we would move away from here. The government of this country said all missionaries must leave at once. If we stay, our lives will be in danger. So we are going for the safety of all of us. Try to understand that. God will take care of your little friend. The Lord knows what is best for us, even if it seems hard."

"But it just isn't fair," answered his daughter.

"Just think, though, Rachel," Susie reminded her, "you will get to see your grandparents and cousins, whom you never saw before. Believe me, there are a lot of cousins! I am sure you will like them all, and Grandpa and Grandma Miller as well as Grandpa and Grandma Eash."

Rachel was still uncertain, but she had no choice. One thing she was sure of—she didn't want her family to go and leave her behind.

"Well then, Mom," she asked, "may I go to Nedra's hut and give her my Mandy?" Mandy was Rachel's rag doll, and she played with it every day. Nedra never had a doll, so Rachel shared and sometimes even let Nedra keep Mandy overnight.

"What? Do you really want to part with Mandy? I thought she was your own special toy," responded her mother.

"She is," Rachel answered, "but Nedra has no

toys at all and lives in that little house. She doesn't even have a bed. I think she would be glad to have Mandy to sleep on the floor with her or in her hammock."

"If you are sure that's what you want to do, then it's all right with me. But be careful and don't stay long. I'll send Mark with you. Go by way of the Chinon well. It is the shortest and safest path."

"I'll go with them," James offered. "It is no longer a wise thing to send the children alone."

"Yes, you are right, and I'll feel better if you are with them," Rebecca agreed.

"Can I play just a little bit with Nedra, Dad?" Rachel begged. "I want to swing in her hammock one more time and make mud pies."

"No, Rachel, you will have to give her your doll and say good-bye as quickly as you can. We must hurry home and get ready."

"Why is everyone so afraid? If Nedra and I can play together and like each other, why can't other people be friends to missionaries?"

"Maybe it's because we can't see through the eyes of a child," replied her dad. Rachel thought that was a strange answer, but she didn't reply for they had reached their destination.

"Here," offered Rachel, placing her Mandy doll in Nedra's arms. "You keep her."

"*Gracias, niña* (thanks, girl)," said Nedra.

"When do you leave?" asked Nedra's mother.

"*Mañana* (tomorrow)," answered James. "Come now," he said, taking his daughter by the hand. Rachel said a tearful good-bye and, without looking back, walked home with her dad.

She slept little that night. Dogs were barking, animals were rustling and screeching in the dark, and gunshots in the distance frightened her. *Why is the night so lonely?* Rachel wondered, as she missed Mandy. She heard a rooster crow, and at last she fell into a fitful sleep.

"Rachel, wake up." Someone was shaking her. Was it morning already? Susie was standing by their bed fully dressed. "Come on, Rachel, we have to hurry." Hurry, hurry, hurry! It seemed that was about all she heard any more, and she did not like it.

"I'll get dressed, but then I think I'll run over and say good-bye to Nedra and Mandy doll one more time."

"No, you can't," her sister informed her. "We just have time for our morning Bible reading and prayer and a bite to eat. Mom said so." It all seemed so unreal.

Soon they were on their way to the airport. The road was rough and dusty, and their driver didn't seem to miss a bump. Finally, they arrived, had their baggage checked, and cleared customs. After a wait, they boarded the plane, found seats, and put on their seat belts. The airliner taxied down the runway, and then they were airborne.

"I'm scared." Rachel shivered, clinging tightly to her mother's arm. "Let's stop. I want to get off. I'm afraid we'll fall." Her sister and her two brothers laughed at Rachel, but her mother consoled her frightened child.

"Don't be afraid, Rachel. Remember the verse we taught you to say. 'What time I am afraid, I will trust in thee.' "

"Well, how long do I have to trust? Will we be there soon?"

"Dear girl," answered Rebecca, "you must learn to trust God always, forever."

"Forever and ever?" Rachel asked.

"Yes," said her mother. "No matter how old we are, the Lord wants us to trust him."

"Oh, does that mean nothing bad will ever happen to me?"

"No, but it does mean that God will help you and all of us, even when some things don't go the way we plan."

"Like not staying where Nedra lives?" Rachel asked.

"Yes, that and many other things. Your father and I had not planned on moving back to the States. But God's ways are better than ours, and God has a purpose in this."

"Are we almost there?" Rachel asked, not understanding the distance.

"It will be a while yet," answered her mother. "I will tell you a story, and then it won't seem to take so long."

Rebecca knew how Rachel loved to hear stories. As a good parent, she wanted to make their journey a pleasant one. Rachel settled back, exclaiming in anticipation, "Oh, goody. Tell me about the coat of many colors."

"That's a long story, Rachel. Maybe I won't be

able to tell all of it before the plane lands."

"Try, Mom, please. I love that story. Even if you can't tell all of it, then just tell part."

The three older children were engrossed in the sights from the plane and the activities of the stewardesses. Meanwhile, Rachel listened intently to her mother's soothing voice. By the time a light lunch was served, Rachel had relaxed and was enjoying herself as much as the rest of the family.

Soon now they would set their feet on the soil of their beloved homeland, and Rachel would be exposed to a way of life totally foreign to her.

3
First Impressions

When the big jet landed in Miami, Rachel was glad. Then her brother Timothy reminded her that they were not yet home.

"Remember, Rachel," he said, "we told you we will fly on two different planes before we get to Ohio." In her excitement, she had forgotten. Her parents had tried to prepare her well for the trip in the short time they had before leaving Central America.

"I don't like this place," Rachel complained. "There are so many people, and it's too noisy. I want to go back home." She clung to her mother in fright.

It was hard to hear one another talk above the din and bustle of people and the constant announcements of incoming or departing flights. Rebecca took her two daughters and made her way to the restrooms. While there she talked with Rachel, trying to still her fears. Susie also tried to comfort her.

"Remember, Rachel, Mom and Dad are with us. They won't let anything happen to you." Small consolation it was, but after waiting in the lounge for a while, Rachel's tears ceased.

"I'm hungry," she stated.

"We'll go to the snack shop then, and find Dad and the boys," Rebecca told the girls. "That is where they said they would be. Maybe we can have a bite to eat."

Rachel couldn't believe all the food she saw displayed there. Some things, like potato chips, she had never tasted. Her parents couldn't believe the prices.

"Maybe we'll just have orange juice or milk," James suggested. "Since we had a light lunch on the plane, I don't suppose anyone is real hungry."

"I'm not," said Mark. "My stomach doesn't feel good."

"Mine neither," Susie added.

"It's probably from flying," James responded. "You all seem tired. I know Mom and I are. And everything is so different here, it's unsettling."

Rachel formed another opinion. "After we get to Ohio, I'll never fly again," she vowed, in childish innocence.

"You are a big *Buppli* (baby)," her brother Mark told her.

"I am not," Rachel defended herself. "Dad, Mark is calling me names. He says I'm a big *Buppli*."

"We are all tired, so let's just try to be patient

with each other. Rachel, you're not a *Buppli*, and Mark, I want no more name-calling."

"She does act *bupplish* though," Mark griped.

"Perhaps when you were her age, you acted the same way," James reminded him.

"Yes," Rachel agreed, "you acted just like me."

"How would you know?" Mark asked.

"Let's just forget it and be glad we are almost through traveling," Rebecca told her children.

At last they heard their flight called. Once more they gathered at the boarding gate, ready for departure.

"You can hold to my hand, Rachel," Susie offered. "Mom has her hands full with the shopping bag and her purse."

"Stay together," James told his family. It was so crowded, and everyone seemed to want to be first on board. Finally, they were airborne again.

"Mom," cried Rachel, "I'm getting sick!" She certainly was. The stewardess brought more airsick bags, and Rebecca was glad she had tissues in the shopping bag.

Rachel seemed to have started a chain reaction. Soon Mark and Timothy had the same problem. It was terribly embarrassing. People turned the other way, and some made rude remarks.

"I can't help it if I have to *kotze* (vomit)," whimpered Rachel.

"I know," said her mother, trying to console her.

The stewardesses were kind and helpful. They supplied wet washcloths and cups of ginger ale to sip.

At five o'clock that evening, they reached the Columbus airport. The Millers were waiting for their son and his family. What a happy meeting that was!

"Thank God you are home safe," cried Grandma Miller.

"Yes, we are thankful," responded James, hugging his mother and then his father, too.

"Rebecca, I'm so glad you are back." James' mother gave her a warm embrace.

"Me, too," said someone else who had just joined them.

"Susan, oh, Susan!" exclaimed Rebecca. "I'm so glad to see you. How nice of you to come."

"I wouldn't have missed it," claimed her dear sister-in-law.

The children had been standing by, waiting to join in the greetings and go wherever it was they were going for the night.

"Oh my, just look at your children," remarked Grandma Miller. "How they have grown! Why, Rebecca Sue, you are almost as tall as your mother. Do they still call you 'Susie'? Timothy, I do believe you are taller than she is. Mark, why, you were only four when you left and here you are eleven. Do you remember us?"

Mark thought he did, but maybe it was just the letters and photos they shared. Since James' parents were Mennonite, they would take pictures, unlike Rebecca's Amish parents.

"Who have we here?" asked Grandma, patting Rachel's head lovingly. "Why, this must be Rachel.

My, my, but you look like your mother used to."

Rachel tried to hide behind her mother's skirt. She didn't like such a fuss. "Come," said Grandma, "don't be afraid of me. I'm your *Grossmammi* (grandmother)." But Rachel buried her face deeper in the folds of her mother's dress.

This was not like Rachel at all. She usually made up easily with people. "I guess she's just tired," explained Rebecca, as she patted her daughter on the head.

"Well, of course," agreed Grandma. "What am I thinking about? Let's get you home and fed and rested up. Then we can talk."

Rachel already decided she wasn't going to like living here. She thought her grandma talked too much, and she whispered that impression to Susie.

"That's just because she's so glad to see us," Susie assured her.

Their first night was spent with James' parents. Rachel missed her Mandy doll. She was used to sleeping with her unless she let Nedra have her for a night. Now she wondered why she had given her away. It was as though she had left part of herself behind.

By morning the family felt rested and refreshed. Rachel began to respond to her grandparents a bit now but was still rather timid. After breakfast James asked, "Could you take us over to Rebecca's folks this morning? I'm sure they are wondering if we are here or still on our way."

"Sure, we will be glad to take you, but you will come back here for the night, won't you?"

"Guess we will wait and see," answered James. "If I know Rebecca's mother, she'll probably insist that we stay there."

When Rachel saw the small *Dawdy Haus* her other grandparents lived in, she was delighted. "Look Mom," she cried with glee, "it's a little house almost like Nedra's. Only it has a real roof and windows. I like it. Oh, can we live here? Can we?"

"It's too small for our family," her mother answered.

The moment Rachel saw her other grandma, she liked her. She stretched out her hands and reached her way right into Ellie's heart. "Oh look, Dawdy," Ellie exclaimed. "My little Becky has come back. She is you all over again, Rebecca," she told her daughter.

Rachel had many first impressions, but this was one she knew she would like to remember.

4

Bittersweets, Sour Grapes, and Persimmons

True to James' prediction, Grandma Eash insisted they stay the night.

"Do you have enough room for us?" Rebecca asked.

"I'll make *Bodde Neschder* (floor nests, beds)."

"I want to stay," said Rachel. "It would be almost like sleeping on the floor with my friend if I could sleep on the floor in your room, Grandma."

Rachel's mother was surprised. Her daughter had been so reluctant in getting acquainted with her other grandparents.

"Why do you want to stay here, Rachel?" her mother asked.

" 'Cause this grandma has a little house that I like, and in that baby chair is a doll almost like my Mandy doll."

Rebecca hadn't noticed the small child's chair in one corner of the big living room, but it caught

Rachel's attention almost right away. "Oh, that," said Grandma Ellie. "I made that *Lumbebopp* (rag doll) so when the grandchildren come the girls will have something to play with. Would you like to hold her, Rachel?"

Rachel just nodded.

"Go get her, then," Grandma told her.

"What's her name?" Rachel asked.

"Ach, I just call her *Lumbebopp*," answered Grandma.

"I'm going to call her Mandy," said Rachel.

It was finally decided that James and the two boys would return to the Miller home for the night, while Rebecca and the girls would stay at David and Ellie's house.

"But I need our night clothes and a few other things," Rebecca pointed out.

"We will see that you get them," said Grandma Miller.

Soon Roy's wife, Lydia, and some of the children came over from the big farmhouse to welcome James and his family back. Rachel was happy to see other girls and boys about her own age. Now she would have new playmates.

"These are your cousins, Rachel," her mother told her.

Lydia insisted that they all come to her place for supper. "You, too," she told James' parents.

"Are you sure that won't be too much for you?" asked Mrs. Miller.

"No, no, I want you to come," Lydia responded.

It all worked out quite well. The Millers took Rebecca to get the things she needed for the night, and then returned with her to eat supper at Roy's house. It was nearing chore time, and Roy told his two sons, Scott and Mervin, to bring the cows from the far pasture.

"Oh, I'd like to see where the cows are," Rachel told her cousin Emma.

"May Rachel and I go, too?" asked Emma, Roy's daughter.

"I suppose so, if it's all right with Rachel's mother," Lydia said.

Rebecca agreed. "I guess it's okay, but don't be a bother, Rachel."

Scott and Mervin were not too willing to have them tag along. "Girls are always *Druwwel* (trouble)," they complained.

As they started out the lane, the boys began to grumble. "I don't see why the girls always have to follow us," Scott remarked.

"I know," said Mervin, "and here comes Mary now, too. She is so poky and can't keep up. Dad doesn't like it if we are late."

"It's all that Rachel girl's fault. She's the one who asked to go along."

"We ought to teach her a lesson. She is so full of questions. Grandma thinks Rachel is so cute. I don't," Mervin declared.

"Neither do I," agreed Scott.

They hadn't gone far when Rachel moaned, "I'm hungry."

"You'll just have to wait till we get home," replied Scott.

"No, she won't," Mervin told him. "Look at those wild grapes by the fence there. Let's give her a bunch."

"Yeah," said Scott, "that ought to take care of her appetite."

"Here, Rachel," her cousin Mervin called. "Look at these reddish balls. They are called wild grapes, and they are free. Have some."

Rachel looked at the cluster of tiny grapes. They were tempting. She reached out and took a handful. She popped a few into her mouth. They were unripe and so sour that she began to spit and cough. The boys laughed and laughed. Rachel and the other girls didn't think it was funny at all.

Along the pasture lane, they came to a persimmon tree. The persimmons weren't ripe yet, but a few had dropped from the tree.

"What are those?" asked Rachel.

"Ask the boys," said Emma. "They'll know."

"Oh," said Scott, seeing his chance to further discourage the girls from following them around, "those are persimmons. If you eat some of those, you will forget all about the sour taste of the wild grapes."

Willingly Rachel picked up a green persimmon and put it into her mouth, biting down hard. What an awful taste! It was ten times worse than the sour grapes had been. It made her mouth feel as if it were drawn shut. Rachel cried and cried. Mary and Emma scolded their brothers for what they had done.

"You knew those things weren't good to eat,

didn't you?" Mary asked her brothers. "I'm telling on you, and then you'll get a spanking. Come on, Rachel, don't believe them any more." Mary put her arm around Rachel and tried to comfort her.

The bittersweet by the wayside was bright with yellow capsules which would soon open to show the orange centers. By now both boys were a bit frightened about their mischievous deeds, so they picked some bittersweet for Rachel. They told her they were like pretty flowers, and she could take them home to Grandma Ellie.

Nothing would have pleased Rachel more, but by this time she did not trust the boys. As they walked across the bridge, she tossed the bittersweet into the little brook below. Later she found out that both of her grandmothers loved bittersweet!

The boys told Rachel to whistle as they got close to their home to show that everyone was having a good time. She discovered, however, that there was no way one could whistle after eating a green persimmon.

The girls did tell their parents.

"I think Scott and Mervin are mean," Rachel declared. "I like Emma and Mary and all of my grandparents. But I hate those boys. I would spank them hard and make them eat a whole plate of sour grapes and those green things for supper," she told her grandmother.

"Rachel, come here," said Grandma Ellie. "You must never hate anyone. The Bible says to hate is the same as killing. The boys shouldn't have done what they did. I'm sure they will be punished. You can hate what they did, but never hate people."

Ellie thought about how much Rachel was like her mother, Rebecca. She had strong feelings and needed guidance.

"Well, I'd make them eat the whole cinnamon tree, then," Rachel remarked. It was plain to see she was still harboring revenge within her heart.

The two boys were dealt with by their father.

"We were just playing a few jokes on her, Dad," Scott told him.

"It's all right to play jokes," Roy told them, "as long as it's not hurtful to the other person. Just remember that. Rachel is a young child, and everything in this country is new to her. We should try to make it easy for her to adjust."

"Why do girls always want to tag along?" Mervin asked.

"That's just the way it is with girls. I don't really know why, but you ought to be glad they think enough of you to want to be where you are."

This was a new thought, and the boys weren't sure how they felt about it. One thing they agreed on was that Rachel was going to be a pest, and they didn't like it.

5

The Amish Way

Everyone was amazed that the Millers had brought so little back with them. The churches held sewings to supply them with clothing. Collections were taken in several congregations.

James found work right away at a sawmill and was used often in Mennonite preaching services. They were able to rent a fairly nice house in the country, only two miles from the sawmill. Two Sunday school classes chipped in and bought a secondhand car for the family.

Timothy and Susie were able to do odd jobs after school and on Saturdays, which was a big help. Susie often helped in neighboring homes as a part-time *Maut* (hired girl), doing baby-sitting and working around the house and garden. Timothy mowed lawns or helped with haying and other farm work. It was a busy time, but the family was grateful for the kindness of dear friends.

"Mom," asked Rachel, "can Grandma make me dresses like Emma and Mary wear? Dresses with little aprons and a cap to wear on my head all the time like they do?"

"Why do you want to dress like that?" asked Susie.

"I just want to. They aren't fancy or anything. I like the way they dress, that's all," Rachel answered.

"We'll see," Rachel's mother told her. "Let's not be a bother to Grandma. You have several new dresses now that the church gave us."

"Oh, I won't be a bother," Rachel promised. "I like Grandma Miller, but Grandma Ellie makes me think of Nedra's mom. She is so plain and fun to be with. My other grandma is fun, too, but I wish I could live close to Grandma Ellie like Uncle Roy's children do."

It was in-between Sunday for Grandpa and Grandma Eash. That meant it was the Sunday when church wasn't held in their district.

"I think I'll invite James and his family for Sunday dinner," Ellie told David.

"Well, suit yourself," Grandpa answered.

She planned and prepared a delicious meal. Rachel was surprised to see that the food was ready for the table as soon as they arrived. "Mammi," she said, "how could you get the dinner ready so quickly after you came home from church?"

"Oh, we didn't go today. It wasn't our church Sunday."

"What does 'church Sunday' mean?" asked Rachel.

"Well, it's the Amish way to have church every other Sunday," replied her grandma. "Then if we want to visit in one of the other congregations, we can.

"You see, we have three large churches around here, but we have no meetinghouses. We have services in our homes every second Sunday. That gives us a chance to visit friends or go to our nearby churches on the Sundays when our own church doesn't meet."

Rachel was learning more about the Amish way of life.

"Don't bother Grossmammi while we are putting the food on the table," Rachel's mother directed.

Rachel pondered this new information. She decided she would ask Emma or Mary if they liked to have church in houses only every other Sunday.

"Oh, yes," answered her cousin Emma, when Rachel brought the question up.

"Why do you like it?"

"Because on the between Sundays, we often have company or else we go to someone else's house for dinner. On church Sundays, we eat our lunch after church right at the house where the preaching was. Then we get to play or hold babies until time to go home."

"What do you have to eat at church?" asked Rachel.

"Oh, in the winter we often have Amish bean soup, peanut butter spread, pickles, pickled red beets, bread, and butter, and the older people have coffee. If we are *glicklich* (lucky) we have corncob molasses."

"Corncob molasses! I never heard of it," exclaimed Rachel. "It doesn't sound good to me."

"Well, it is, though," Emma told her, and Mary agreed. "I know," added Emma, "why don't you ask your mom if you can come overnight some time and go to church with us?"

"Oh, I hope I can. I'll ask her today," Rachel exclaimed.

What a meal they had! The Miller children couldn't remember seeing so much food at one time.

"Ach, I just made the usual," Grandma replied to the remarks of "so much." The usual was a large plate of fried chicken, mounds of mashed potatoes with valleys of browned butter, gravy, peas, stuffing, macaroni salad, date pudding, apple pie, and coffee.

"I guess the poor people would be glad if they could have just one piece of chicken," said Rachel. "I know, I'll save a piece and send it to Nedra."

"Oh, no, you couldn't do that," her mother told her.

"Why not? Nedra would be so happy."

"It would spoil before it got there, and Nedra wouldn't like the taste. It would make her sick."

"Your grandma would know what that is like," said Grandpa. "She once almost ate a sandwich which even yet makes her almost sick to think about."

"Tell me, Grandma, please," begged Rachel.

"Maybe while we do the dishes, but not now," Grandma answered.

"I'll help with the dishes then," Rachel volunteered.

"My, my," exclaimed Susie. "You don't offer to help at home. We almost have to push you into the dishpan."

"You don't tell me stories when we work like Grandma does."

"This is our Amish way of teaching the children," said Grandma. "We don't hold to Sunday school, but we feel it's a privilege and God-given duty to teach our children at home."

"You don't have Sunday school?" asked Rachel.

"No, child, we don't."

"Why not?" Rachel inquired.

"One reason is because we fear parents may think that they don't need to teach their children, that it's the Sunday school's job."

"Well, I like when you teach me. My mom teaches me, too, and so does Sister Carol at Sunday school. I ought to learn a lot. But now tell me about the sandwich."

"Ach, Rachel, I almost forgot," said Grandma.

"My brothers used to do a lot of trapping. They caught a skunk once and hung the hide and fur in our smokehouse. We had all the hams and sausages in there to cure. I was home alone one day. When lunchtime came, I was hungry for fresh sausage. So I went to the smokehouse and sliced off a nice piece of meat. I noticed a strong odor.

"While the meat was cooking, the bad smell got stronger. But I was so hungry I made a sandwich with it anyway. One bite was enough for me. *Skunk,*

I thought as I bit into it. I spit it out right away. The smell of that skunk had ruined all our meat. For a long time, I did not care for sausage."

"Oh," said Rachel, "what happened to your brothers?"

"They were told never to put furs from trapping in the smokehouse again, and to take a lesson from that."

"What lesson?" asked Rachel.

"Just as the odor of that skunk ruined our meat, so easy can the ways of the world rub off on us if we aren't careful."

"What are the ways of the world?" Rachel wondered.

"All things that are wrong," answered Grandma. "Such as lying, stealing, overeating, being proud, pleasing ourselves instead of God."

"I don't ever want to be like the world, Grandma. I want to be like you and learn Amish. Can you make me Amish clothes so I can come stay overnight with Emma and Mary and go to church with them?"

Grandma was so pleased. "If it's all right with your mother," she told Rachel, "it's all right with me."

"What is my little chatterbox begging for now?" Rebecca asked, as she and Lydia came from carrying leftover food to the basement and pantry.

"She wants me to make her an Amish outfit, and I'd be glad to," Grandma said.

6

Cookies, Crackers, and Cute Babies

Rachel had her ninth birthday the year after her family came back from Central America. Her Grandma thought this would be a good time to make Amish clothes as a nice gift for her.

Homesickness for her little friend Nedra had plagued Rachel, so it was just what she needed when it was decided to let her spend several days with Grandpa and Grandma Eash.

"I don't see why you want to dress Amish," chided her sister, Susie.

"Because I like Mammi and Dawdy and my cousins Emma and Mary," Rachel replied.

"Well, I like them, too, but I'd rather wear clothes with zippers than with straight pins."

"Emma and Mary don't use straight pins. They have buttons down the back of their dresses and aprons."

"Only until they are older," said Susie. "When

they are old enough for *Rumschpringe* (running around with other young folks), then they will go from buttons to pins."

"I don't care," answered Rachel.

"Suit yourself then, but you just wait. I bet you will change your mind," predicted Susie.

Rachel flounced out of the room with her head held high. She just knew she would not be sorry. Besides, this would give her a chance to play with Roy's children while Grandma sewed her new clothes. Grandma could have used Mary's pattern, for she and Rachel were nearly the same size, but she wanted an excuse to have her granddaughter for a few days.

Rachel had often begged to be allowed to go along to Amish church one Sunday with her cousins. Thus, it was agreed that she would spend Friday night and all day Saturday with Grandma and Grandpa Eash so Grandma could make her new clothes. Then she would stay Saturday night and go along to church the next morning.

"This will be our birthday present to you," her mother told her.

"It is the bestest birthday present I've ever had. Thank you, oh, thank you," Rachel exclaimed.

"You be sure and listen to Mammi and don't *babble* (chatter) all the time," her mother admonished her.

"Oh, I won't *babble*," promised Rachel. Scott and Mervin thought that's all she did. They tried to avoid her, but it seemed that every time they turned around, Rachel and their two sisters were there. At least on Sunday Rachel, Emma, and Mary went to church in Grandpa's buggy.

Rachel's new dress and cap fit her perfectly. Roy's wife, Lydia, had braided Rachel's hair and put up the braids just like her own young daughters'. It felt strange to Rachel. But she didn't mind at all because she was so pleased to look just as her cousins did.

What fun it was riding along in the buggy! She sat on a little bench in the front buggy box with Emma. Mary sat on Grandma's lap, and Grandpa drove.

"You look just like us," said Emma.

"Yes," agreed Mary, "it seems like you were always a little Amish *Meedel* (girl)."

They giggled and chattered as they drove along. "Oh, there are so many things to see," remarked Rachel. "I never notice so many things when we go to church."

"That's because you go too fast," answered Grandpa.

"Well, I'm going to ask my dad to buy us a horse and buggy. Then we can go slower to church and see more nice things," Rachel informed them.

"We are almost there, girls," said Grandma Ellie. "Now you must settle down and not *rutsche* (squirm) in church."

"May I sit on your lap when we go home?" Rachel asked. "Then I can see better yet."

"Yes, I suppose so," Grandma answered.

Buggies were coming from all directions. Everyone seemed to be dressed alike, Rachel noticed, as they stepped down from the buggy. She stayed close to Grandma and her cousins.

They entered the house and were seated on backless benches in the kitchen. A hush seemed to fall over everyone. Soon the singing began, but Rachel could understand only a few words. The Scripture reading and preaching were also in German. Her mother had taught her Pennsylvania Dutch, but this was different.

She wondered why they didn't go to the children's classes and started to ask Emma in a whisper. Grandma nudged her and shook her head. Rachel began to wonder if she had done a wise thing in coming to the Amish meeting. Just then something happened to lift her spirits and quench her doubts.

The lady of the house entered the room with one bowl of nice round, homemade cookies and another of soda crackers. She began to pass these around, and mothers with babies and young children took some. Rachel could hardly wait until her turn came. The cookies reached Emma first, but she didn't take any. Rachel's heart sank. Wouldn't she be allowed to have any either? Mary, however, took a cookie and two cracker squares.

Rachel looked at Mammi, who nodded and smiled, so she gratefully took of the goodies. Later she learned that one who has turned eleven is too old to eat cookies and crackers in church. Rachel was glad she wasn't eleven. For her this was the best part of the service.

Later the *Hausfraa* (housewife) came with a pitcher of nice cool water and a tin cup. She poured water into the cup and gave it to the woman at the end of the bench, who then passed it down the line. When the cup was empty, it was given back to the lady with the pitcher for a refill. Everyone drank from the same cup.

Rachel wondered why everyone looked so solemn. Many people were blowing their noses and wiping tears. Was it because of what the preacher was saying? He spoke so forcefully and sternly. Rachel noticed her grandma wiping tears. She didn't like for him to make Mammi cry. Little did she know that the tears were of concern for the many who had strayed from their fold, and that Grandma Ellie was thinking of her own dear Rebecca.

Finally, after three hours, church was over. Now Rachel was to experience an Amish church meal.

"What is this that you spread on my bread?" she asked Mammi.

"Did you like it?" Grandma asked.

"Oh, yes, I want more."

"That's corncob molasses," Emma told her. "And you thought you wouldn't like it."

After the meal, the women and men visited while the children played. "Let's see if we can *knutsche* (cuddle) babies," Mary told Rachel.

"Oh, I hope we can. They are so cute. But why do some of the girl babies wear little capes and others don't?" asked Rachel.

"All the girl babies do wear capes. The boy babies don't wear them," answered Mary.

"But all the babies are wearing dresses," remarked Rachel.

"Sure," Mary told her. "All the boy babies wear dresses, too, until they are out of diapers.

"Oh, well," Rachel responded, "they are all cute babies anyway. Let's see if we can *knutsche* any of them."

They soon found mothers who gladly relinquished the care of their little ones to them. "When I'm married and have *schnuck Bupplin* (cute babies)," said Rachel, "I'm going to make them be Amish and take them to church where they can have cookies and crackers, too."

"And even corncob molasses," Mary said, laughing.

7
Outrunning My Shoes

Time moved on. The next summer Rachel was ten.

"Mom, can I stay over with Uncle Roy's girls Saturday night and go to church with them on Sunday?" she asked her mother.

"Don't you like going to church with us?" her mom asked her.

"Yes, I do, but there's just something I like about their way."

Rebecca remembered her own struggles years before when she left the Amish. Sometimes that longing still haunted her. "We'll ask your dad. But tell me, can you understand the preaching?"

"Not nearly all of it, but I can learn," answered her daughter. "I learned Spanish easily."

"Sure," Rebecca told her, "but that's because you were born in a Spanish-speaking country. You had a little Spanish playmate and picked it up from her."

"I'll pick German up from my cousins, too, or at least I'll try."

"But they talk Pennsylvania Dutch, not German," Rebecca reminded her.

"That's right," Rachel responded. "So I'll get Dawdy to start teaching me to read the German Bible and the prayer book. Then I'll catch more from the preaching and the hymns."

Rachel's parents decided she could go this time, and she was excited.

"What do you think I should wear?" Rachel asked her sister, Susie. The clothes her Grandma had made for her were too small by this time.

"Wear what you want to. They will think you are worldly no matter what. I don't understand why you want to go at all!"

"Don't you like Grandpa and Grandma or Roy's family and our cousins?" Rachel asked.

"Sure I do," replied Susie, "but I have friends in our church, and at least I know what's being said."

"I'll learn to understand better. Mary claims she can tell more and more what they are saying as she gets older."

"Do as you please, but don't ask me what to wear," Susie stated.

Susie had to admit to herself that she admired many things about the Amish. She liked their quiet, unhurried way of life. They were generally friendly and willing to help in a time of need. But unlike her sister, Rachel, Susie didn't think she would care to dress in such a plain, drab fashion.

Scott and Mervin were not excited at all when

they learned that Rachel was coming to spend the night and go to Sunday services. It wasn't that they didn't like their cousin, but every time she came, the girls tagged along with them. The boys were almost old enough for *Rumschpringe*, going out with other youth to singings. They felt way too grown-up for their younger sisters and Rachel.

A plan began to form in the minds of the boys as to how they might discourage the girls from following them around. On Saturday evening after supper, they told the girls they were going to visit the neighbors. They well knew that the girls would want to go with them.

Instead of going to the neighbors' farm, the boys ran down the road a ways and hid in the ditch. It was nearly dark, but soon they heard the girls coming down the road, just as they expected. *Now for some fun,* they thought. Rustling in the grass, they began making weird noises.

"What was that?" asked Emma, stopping in her tracks.

"I don't know," Mary answered.

"Maybe it's just a cat or something," Rachel remarked.

All was quiet now, so the girls started on down the road. There it was again, a strange screeching and stirring in the ditch.

"Run!" ordered Emma.

"No," Rachel said. "If we run it will know we are afraid and will chase us for sure. Let's just walk fast."

All three girls turned and started for home. Then

47

they heard a sound of someone following them. They stopped and looked back but could see no one. When they paused, they no longer heard anyone either. Clasping hands with each other, they began to walk on. Now they heard it once more. They walked faster, and the footsteps they heard also walked faster.

"Let's run!" Emma again gasped in panic, and this time all three took off as fast as they could. But whatever they heard made sounds of running after them just as fast.

Rachel couldn't keep up with Emma and Mary, and their hands were clasped no longer. It was each one for herself. Rachel, being the last to reach the house, ran panting into the kitchen, where her two cousins stood white-faced and trembling.

"We thought it caught you," Mary told Rachel.

"No," panted Rachel, "but it followed me all the way to the house."

"I wonder what it was," said Emma, puzzled.

"I don't know, but I hope it didn't get the boys," Mary remarked. "I'm really frightened."

After a while Scott and Mervin came home. They had seen the girls run and had enjoyed a good laugh. Innocently, they entered the kitchen and, trying to keep straight faces, asked the girls what they had been doing all evening.

After hearing the story of their frightful escape, the boys could keep quiet no longer. "So we scared you, did we?" they joked.

"Was that you hiding in the ditch and making noises?" asked Rachel.

"Then you chased us home yet and really tried to scare us," accused Emma.

"I don't think that's funny," Rachel declared.

All three girls started chasing after the boys. As they began running over the porch and down the stairs, Rachel was suddenly aware of something. She heard those footsteps again, following her. She stopped, and so did the sound of other steps.

"What's wrong, Rachel?" Scott asked. "You ready to admit you can't catch us?"

"No," Rachel answered, "but listen. Whenever I run, I hear someone or something following me. When I stop, it stops. Just listen." She began to run again. They all heard it.

"Let's go inside," said Mervin. He suspected something. Inside by the lamplight, he directed, "Lift up your feet, Rachel."

Now they saw what had caused the problem. One of Rachel's shoe soles was coming apart. Whenever she walked fast or ran, it sounded as if someone else were following in her steps. Suddenly it seemed funny to everyone, and Rachel laughed along with the rest of them.

"It still wasn't nice of you to scare us in the first place, though," said Rachel.

After that evening she was teased many times about how she tried to outrun her shoes.

Grandma used even this experience to teach a truth. "Remember, Rachel, we can never outrun the attacks of Satan. You girls should not have followed the boys without permission."

Rachel knew Grandma was right.

It turned out, though, that Rachel had a pleasant visit to the Amish church service in a nearby home. Mary let her borrow an Amish dress, cape, and apron, plus a black cap, to wear to the meeting.

Rachel felt as though she belonged, and she tried to listen carefully to the ministers. She felt the close-knit fellowship of this people. Once more she pledged within her heart to be one with them some day.

8
Impressing Company!

By the summer when Rachel was eleven, she had learned to work as all Amish and Mennonite girls do. Many times she would help her mom or her grandma with cleaning, garden work, or whatever task needed doing. That's how it came about one day that she baked pies for her grandma.

Grandma Ellie was visiting at James and Rebecca's home. She told Rachel, "We are expecting company for Sunday dinner. I have to clean and bake and wash some bedding. It hurries me so, and I can't work as fast as I used to."

"We can bake the pies for you, Mammi," Rachel offered. "Why, I can bake them here at our house and bring them over by Saturday noon. Can't I, Mom?" she asked her mother.

"I don't know why not, if we know what kind you want," Rebecca answered.

"Oh, but that's too much trouble," Grandma said.

"No, it won't be any trouble at all," insisted Rachel.

"I'll need to bring the stuff over here which you'll need, or else I'll pay for it," said Grandma.

"No, you needn't do that. Just tell us what kind you want," Rebecca responded.

"Well, what is handy for you?"

"Oh, I can make any kind you would like," Rachel assured her.

"Do you have any canned raspberries yet?" asked Grandma.

"Yes, I'm sure we do," Rebecca answered.

"Well then, if Rachel wants to make two raspberry pies, I'll give you a jar of raspberries back."

On Saturday Rachel hurried with her usual duties of cleaning so she could get started on the pies for Mammi. She had no sooner begun than out-of-state visitors arrived. The ladies of the house were glad that at least most of their cleaning was done.

Rebecca took her guests into the living room. As she went, she instructed Rachel, "Make sure you get everything put together right."

"I will," Rachel told her. Why need her mother worry? She had baked pies at least twice before. Today she felt grown-up, and, yes, quite proud also, to be left alone in the kitchen with the baking. The dough was on the counter top to be rolled out. To make sure the company knew what she was doing, Rachel banged and pounded the rolling pin as hard as she could.

Soon her mother came to the kitchen to see what was going on. "Rachel, must you make all that noise? Please try to be quieter and roll the dough gently and evenly."

"Yes, Mom, I will," she promised. From then on, it was much more peaceful in the kitchen, but Rachel wondered if their guests knew she was baking all by herself.

She had a terrible time putting the dough into the pie tins. It broke in many places, and she tried to patch it up as well as she could. The filling, too, was thin and runny, but she reasoned that when it was baked, it would thicken.

Her sister, Susie, came in from the outdoors, where she had been weeding flower beds. "You sure make a mess when you bake," she told Rachel.

"I'm just ready to clean it up," Rachel said. "See, these pies are ready to bake. Will you open the oven door for me?" she asked, carefully picking up a pie and bringing it to the stove.

As Susie opened the oven door, she remarked, "Goodness, Rachel, the top crust on your pie looks like a patchwork quilt. What were you doing, playing with it?"

"No," answered Rachel. "The dough was hard to work with. It kept tearing all the time. I did the best I could."

"It sounded for a while as if you were hammering something," remarked Susie. Seeing the pained look on her sister's face, Susie added, "They'll probably taste better than they look, and that's the important thing, sis." She gave Rachel an affectionate pat on the head.

That in itself lifted Rachel's spirits, and she felt

better. But not for long. Soon the smell of something burning filled the air. The odor drifted into the living room, and Rachel's mother excused herself from her company and came hurrying into the kitchen.

"Rachel, what are you doing?" she asked her daughter.

"Just baking," Rachel replied.

But as Rebecca opened the oven door, black smoke poured out into the room. "Ach my!" exclaimed Rachel. "I made them too full. I wanted big, fat pies for Dawdy's company; now they will only be skinny ones."

Some of the pie filling had dripped to the bottom of the oven and was burning to a crisp. Mother had told her earlier not to fill the pies too full or they were liable to boil over. She mentally scolded herself for not listening.

The company had to move to the porch to continue visiting. Mother set the pies out until later. She was able to clean the oven and place a cake pan with water under the tins to catch any more spills.

Rachel was so embarrassed.

"Who is our company, anyway?" Susie asked her.

"I don't know, but I wish they wouldn't have come," she sobbed, with tears running down her cheeks. "Now they will think I'm dumb and don't even know how to bake pies."

"I don't know who they are, Rachel, but I'm sure they didn't come to find out if you can bake," Susie told her.

James called his daughters out to the porch. Rachel wished she could run and hide, but Susie told her to come along. They were introduced to Roman Schrock and his wife, Louella.

"These folks came all the way from Oregon. They are related to us. Roman is my second cousin on my father's side," James explained. The girls shook hands politely.

"Which one of you was the busy cook in the kitchen?" Louella inquired.

Rachel wished she wouldn't have asked! Hanging her head, she barely whispered, "I was."

"Well, now," remarked Louella, "you needn't feel bad. I'm a lot older than you are, and many times I've had the same problem with pies as you did. Isn't that right, Roman?"

"Sure is," her husband said, laughing. Rachel felt better, and she liked them right away.

After supper the two pies were delivered to Grandpa's. Grandma had a jar of raspberries, some flour, sugar, and lard to send along back, and she also handed a shiny quarter to Rachel.

"But Grandma," Rachel protested, "the pies are too skinny, and Susie said they look like patchwork."

"They will probably taste good anyway," Grandma assured her.

"You see," Susie told her, "Rachel tried to impress our company by pounding and banging the dough instead of carefully rolling it out. It was very hard to work with."

"It never pays to show off," said Grandma. "The

Bible says that pride goes before a fall. God will humble the proud."

"What do you mean?" asked Rachel.

"Oh, the Lord might let something happen to show us we are no better than others. Sometimes God will shame us to make us humble."

Rachel never did find out what happened to her pies. Although they tasted all right, Mammi could not serve one nice piece to her guests. She borrowed some pies from Lydia, her daughter-in-law. So the visitors were not impressed by Rachel's work after all.

But Dawdy loved the pies and finished eating them, crumbs and all, over the next few days.

9

Weight on the Buggy

Spring had come the next year, and garden planting time drew near. Grandma and Grandpa Eash still liked to have their own small garden, but they were getting along in years.

"You need not put out a garden," Roy's wife told Ellie. "We will have plenty for everyone, no more than you and Dawdy need."

"But I think it's good for us to do what we can, rather than just sit around. Besides, I thought maybe Rachel could spend the summer, if Rebecca can spare her. She is a big help in many ways. Dawdy and I wouldn't be lonesome, and I could teach her a lot, too," Grandma reasoned.

Lydia just smiled. She knew Grandma was thinking up an excuse to have her granddaughter stay awhile. It was hard to imagine her being lonesome with Roy's children living right next door. Lydia sensed that the special bond between Rachel and her grandmother was a beautiful thing. So she said no more.

Grandma approached Rebecca about the possibility of having Rachel for the summer. Her daughter hesitated. "Just let me think it over first, and I will see what James says. Yes, I could spare her, but let's not say a word to Rachel yet. That girl wouldn't give me a moment's peace."

"No, no, I wouldn't," promised Grandma.

"Do you know what Rachel told me the other day?" Rebecca asked.

"With Rachel, I can't imagine. She has many ideas. Some are good, and some need explaining."

"Well, she said, 'When I grow up, I'm going to be Amish.' "

"Did she really?" asked Grandma Ellie.

"Yes, she did."

"And how do you feel about that?" asked Grandma.

"She is such a young girl yet and could change her mind several times. To James and me, it wouldn't matter. All we want is for her to grow up to be a sincere Christian woman."

That's how it came to be, after James and Rebecca gave it much thought, that Rachel spent most of the summer at Grandpa Eash's. She was delighted.

Generally, on weekends she would go home and attend Sunday school and church with her parents. But occasionally she would stay over and go to Amish church. As a twelve-year-old, she was too old for the cookies and crackers passed during church. Nevertheless, she looked forward to those times.

One Sunday afternoon when Rachel had stayed over, she and some of Roy's children asked Grandpa to tell them a story about the "olden days," as they put it.

"Wait until Mammi and I have taken our afternoon nap," suggested Grandpa. "You young ones run and play a while, but far enough from the house so we can't hear noise." He thought perhaps they would forget by then about storytelling, although he rather liked their attention.

"But that's so long to wait," complained Rachel. "Can't you tell us a story first and then rest?"

"Rachel," answered Grandma, "you must learn to be patient. It is good for us to wait sometimes. Maybe it is hard, but there are reasons for us to give up having what we want right away. It helps us to consider other people.

"If we can't wait for others or for what we want, how can we learn to wait upon the Lord until he sees the time is right to give us what we ask?"

"Yes, Mammi," agreed Rachel, "I know you are right. I'm sorry I was so impatient."

"Come on," said Scott, "let's go play in the haymow." They all liked the big rope swing fastened to the track just under the ridge of the roof. One could swing from one side of the barn to the other. What a thrill! The boys did this without any fear at all, but the girls screamed with some apprehension and yet also with delight.

After a while, Roy came from the house and joined his children tussling in the mow. He pushed them several times on the swing, then got the boys interested in pitching horseshoes. The girls decided to make hollyhock flower dolls. All they needed were two flowers and a straight pin.

"They're not as nice as my Mandy *Lumbebopp* (rag doll) that Mammi made," remarked Rachel.

"No, but look how their skirts stand out so," answered Mary.

"It's too much like an *englisch* dress," Rachel said. "So fancy and worldly."

"Now you sound like my mom," Emma told her. "It seems you think Amish is better."

"I do," Rachel replied emphatically, "and some day I'm going to be Amish just like you!"

After they played for an hour, Grandma called from the front porch, "Come now, we are ready for you."

"Have you had your nap?" Rachel asked.

"Ach, *ya* (oh, yes), and I've popped some corn for everyone already."

"Oh, goody," commented Rachel. She ran to the outdoor hand pump and was the first one in line to wash up. The water from the well was cool on their flushed faces.

Grandma was sitting on the porch swing beside Grandpa and polishing apples until they sparkled. Rachel squeezed between them on the swing, and the other children gathered around on the floor, the porch railing, and the steps.

Scott whispered to Mervin, "That little tagalong Mennonite thinks she owns Grandpa."

"She doesn't," Mervin assured him.

"Now, Dawdy, tell us a story," begged Rachel.

"Ach, Rachel," said Grandpa teasingly, "I figured you forgot all about storytelling."

"No, I didn't. Tell us when you were a boy."

Just then Roy's wife came outside to make sure the children weren't bothering Mammi and Dawdy.

"Come on over," invited Grandma. "Dawdy is just fixing to tell one of his stories. Here, have some popcorn."

"Well, I really shouldn't stay. Maybe just a little while. It will soon be chore time."

"Hurry, Dawdy," begged Rachel, "I can't wai—" She caught her flow of words just in time. Grandpa knew what she was about to say, but she had remembered what her Grandma had told her earlier about being impatient. She clasped her hand over her mouth in dismay.

Grandpa's eyes twinkled as he said, "Rachel, since you were about to say wait—"

"But I didn't quite say it," she reminded Dawdy.

"I know, and you did well to remember, but I'll tell you a story about weight on the buggy," he chuckled.

"Now, mind you, this didn't happen to me, but I know the man it did happen to. He sold his farm and bought a smaller place from people who were not Amish. Therefore, he had no buggy shed, not even a barn where he could keep his buggy. One of his neighbors was kind enough to let him keep his horse in his barn.

"Whenever it rained or snowed, the buggy sat outside unprotected from the weather. There was a garage on the property, and he had tried to put his buggy in the garage. But he said either the top of the buggy was just a bit too high or the garage roof was too low.

"One day this man Seth got an idea. Now Seth's wife was a hefty woman."

"What was her name?" inquired Rachel.

"Don't interrupt," Scott told her.

"Oh, she was called Anna," answered Dawdy. "Anyway, Seth told her to get into the buggy; he wanted to try something. She did as he told her. Then Seth put a large stone in the front buggy box, picked up the shafts, and pulled the buggy into the garage without any trouble.

"His problem was solved, and they both laughed at how simple it was. Seth told me it pays to have a good cook and a fat wife. It added just enough weight on the buggy that he got it inside."

"Did that really happen?" asked Rachel.

"Yes, it really did," Dawdy replied, still chuckling.

"I'd just build a bigger garage and not be so fat," Rachel decided.

10

A Tale
of Two Cows

Near the end of milking time each morning,
Rachel had a regular errand. She took the little
stainless steel pail to get fresh milk for Dawdies. It
was a cute imitation of a real milk pail. This one,
though, held only two quarts and had a little lid.
Rachel was glad to fetch good, fresh milk, for she
liked its nice, creamy taste on her oatmeal.

One day she skipped happily along until she
came to the barn door. There she stopped in bewil-
derment. Loud scolding was coming from within.
She heard the sound of a strap hitting an animal. A
cow was bawling.

Rachel didn't know what to do. Should she go
into the barn or run back to the house with an
empty pail?

Then she heard Roy's son Albert say, "I've taken
just about enough from you *alte Kuh* (old cow)!
Spill all the milk, will you? Kick me in my arm?

Well, you won't do it again. Take that, and that, you dumb old thing!" He hit her again and again.

Frightened, Rachel ran as fast as she could back to the *Dawdy Haus*.

"*Was ist letz* (what is wrong)?" asked Mammi. She could see the girl was upset.

"Albert is beating one of the cows with a strap, and the cow is bawling. I was too scared to go in the barn for milk. Oh, Mammi, I think he's killing the cow," Rachel blurted out tearfully.

"No, he won't kill her, but he should not hit her like that or be so angry. None of Roy's cows are kickers. Something must be wrong. I'll send Dawdy out right away."

The rest of the menfolk had finished chores in the barn and were in the hog shed, granary, and various other places. They were not aware of what was taking place between Albert and the cow.

Rachel headed back to the barn, holding onto Grandpa's hand all the way. By now, as they approached the barn, everything was quiet. Albert's face was still flushed, and the back of his neck was actually red. David also noticed some marks across Bessie's back; she was quivering.

"Here, Rachel, give me the pail, and I'll fill it for you." Grandpa dipped warm, strained milk from the ten-gallon can and sent his granddaughter on her way to the house.

"What was going on here, Albert?" Grandpa asked.

"Who said anything was going on?" Albert replied.

"Rachel did. She came out for our milk and heard you beating one of the cows and yelling. It frightened her so badly she came back and told us."

"That tattletale. Why doesn't she stay with her parents where she belongs? She says she wants to be Amish. Ha!" Albert remarked.

"Never mind about Rachel. I asked you a question, and I don't like your rebellious attitude." Generally all the grandchildren were respectful to Dawdy and Mammi, but Albert was still angry.

"Bessie kicked twice for me. Once she hurt my arm, and the last time she spilled most of the milk."

"She doesn't usually kick," said Grandpa, "so something must be wrong. Besides, it won't help to lose your temper." He talked a while longer with his grandson, trying in a firm yet kind way to show the boy that two wrongs don't make a right.

"Let me see your fingernails," Dawdy said.

"What?" asked Albert.

"Your nails—let me take a look. Yes, just as I thought. They're quite long and ragged and probably hurt Bessie. I suggest you cut them and remember animals don't realize why they are being punished. I won't say anything to your dad about this. Let's consider it settled."

"Yes, if that blabbermouth Rachel won't tell," Albert responded.

"I'll talk to her, but I don't want you calling her names. She had to make a big adjustment moving from the place she was born and had lived in for seven years. Try to be understanding, for her and all of our sakes."

Rachel was sad all day because she felt sorry for Bessie. She also felt bad about Albert's temper. Grandma thought it might cheer Rachel up if she told Rachel that they were going to town the next day.

Rachel loved to ride with Grandma and Grandpa in the buggy, and she looked forward to the trip. When she was smaller, many times she sat on the little bench in the front buggy box, just like her grandmother did when she was growing up. Now she was too big for that and had to sit on her grandma's lap. She tried to support herself a bit with her arms so she wouldn't be too heavy.

Rachel was glad they were going into town, but she still wasn't her usual happy self. On the way she again brought up the subject of Albert's behavior.

"Well," said Grandpa, "since you can't get it out of your mind, I will tell you a tale of two cows. I am sure Albert feels bad now because of what he did. In the story I'm going to tell you, two sisters also felt sorry for mistreating two cows. At the time, they thought they were just going to have some fun. They didn't realize how cruel their act would be."

"How can girls be cruel?" asked Rachel. "Now, if you were talking about boys. . . ."

"Well, they just didn't know how much it would hurt the cows. It was a humid summer day, and these girls were sunburned, especially their necks and faces. The flies were bothersome, and at evening milking time the cows switched their tails to keep the flies away. Whenever their tails switched across the girls' necks or faces, it hurt badly.

"No matter how much fly spray they used, the flies came back. After they were finished milking and were alone in the barn, they had an idea. Before turning the last two cows out to pasture, they tied their tails together. Then they stood back to watch what would happen if the cows couldn't switch for a minute.

"The problem was, the girls had tied a knot the only way they knew how—a slipknot. The harder the cows pulled, the tighter the knot became. The cows began to bawl, and finally one cow jerked so hard she actually skinned the other's tail.

"Then one frightened girl said to her sister, *'Mach schnell, grieg die Schmier* (hurry, get the salve)!'

"The other said, 'What will happen when Dad finds out?' "

"Did their dad find out?" asked Rachel.

"Not for a long time," answered Dawdy. "He never could figure out what happened to Bossy's tail. He guessed that she had caught it in a fence. Years later the girls told him about it and how sorry they were. They didn't mean to hurt those two cows.

"But remember, Rachel, foolish acts can never come to any good. Animals aren't like people. They can't reason things out."

"Oh, Grandpa, I'll remember this story and never be unkind to animals."

"I'm glad you feel that way, Rachel," Grandma

said. "Some children seem to think it's great fun to play tricks on helpless creatures. You told me you learned the verse about being kind and tenderhearted, and I think that doesn't only mean to people."

"Is that why you don't carry a buggy whip like some people do?"

"We don't feel we need a whip for our horse. If we want her to go a little faster, all we need to do is say 'giddyap' or tap her gently with the lines," answered Grandpa.

"Well, I bet Doll is glad she's your horse. When I am Amish and have a horse, I don't want a whip either," Rachel decided.

David and Ellie looked at each other and smiled. They were glad Rachel's heart was so tender.

Grandpa had some things to pick up at the hardware store. Mammi took Rachel along first to the dry goods place, where she bought some black organdy for new head coverings for Roy's girls.

"I'd like if you made one for me, too," Rachel told her.

"Well, then I'll just buy a fourth of a yard more," Mammi said. Rachel was pleased. By the time she helped her grandma shop for a few groceries and carry them to the buggy, Dawdy was waiting.

"How about some ice-cream cones?" he asked.

This was a rare treat, and they tasted so good. After they reached home, Rachel felt much better, and she had new truths to ponder.

11
Feathers in the Living Room

Grandma Ellie was all aflutter with delight.

Rachel could tell she was happy, but she didn't know why.

"Why are you so excited?" Rachel asked her grandma.

"Oh, I just got a letter in the mail today saying my sister Fannie and her family are coming to visit. They have two single girls at home yet. Fannie likes things just so, you know, spick-and-span. Her daughters are the same way.

"I know it's better that way than to have things cluttered up. But I haven't even finished the painting that we wanted to get done this summer. Fannie and the girls notice everything." Mammi allowed herself a slight frown.

"I'll help you," Rachel offered.

"That's kind of you, but I'm afraid it's a bigger job than we can handle," Grandma replied.

"Maybe Dawdy can help us, too," suggested Rachel, trying to ease Grandma's mind.

"Ach, he will help me, but he goes so *schusslich* (carelessly) sometimes when he gets in a hurry. Once in a while he says it isn't necessary or he has other things to do, important work. I get the feeling he really doesn't want to help me."

"Oh, Grandma," said Rachel, "don't say that. You know Dawdy wants to help."

Rachel didn't like to hear anything against her dear grandpa. Rachel remembered her Spanish friend Nedra's parents. Many times they would become angry and shout loudly at each other. She never wanted Dawdies or her parents to do that. Rachel often felt sorry for Nedra and thought of how frightened the children were at those times.

"What's wrong, Rachel?" asked Grandma, seeing a look of terror on her face.

"I don't want you and Grandpa to yell at each other like Nedra's mom and dad did," answered the frightened girl.

"Ach, my, no!" exclaimed Grandma, "of course, we won't. I didn't mean to upset you. Grandpa and I don't always agree, but we would never yell at each other or fight. If we don't get the painting done, it won't be the end of the world."

"Grandma, you mentioned something this morning about picking some green beans for supper. I'll go do that now, and you can rest a while," offered Rachel.

"I could take a little nap," agreed Ellie.

By the time Grandma woke up, Rachel had

picked and washed the beans. She got two pans and settled herself by the kitchen table to snip the ends off.

"Why don't we go out under a shade tree to do this?" Grandma suggested.

"That's a good idea. It would be cooler," Rachel agreed.

Taking their chairs and pans, they made their way to the front lawn. Soon several of Roy's children joined them. Snip-snap went the bean ends as they worked. Rachel liked the sound of the ping, ping, as she dropped each crisp bean into her metal bowl.

"Let's sing while we do the beans," Rachel suggested. She loved it when the families gathered and sang beautiful hymns, both English and German.

"Oh, I'd rather have Grandma tell us a story," said Mary. "She knows so many and we learn a lot of lessons from them."

"Why can't we do both?" asked Rachel.

"It won't take that long to do these beans," replied Grandma. She didn't think it wise always to give in to Rachel, so she added, "Why don't I tell a story now, and then tonight after supper you all come to our house and we will sing."

That pleased everyone, so Grandma told a story. "Once long ago," she began, "my mother got a letter in the mail from her aunt Polly. The letter said Aunt Polly's family was coming to visit."

"Why, that's just like the letter you got from your sister Fannie," remarked Rachel.

"Yes, and Aunt Polly and my sister were much

alike. Both quite particular. Aunt Polly lived in Indiana."

"Were they going to come all that way by horse and buggy?" Rachel asked, naturally curious.

"No, they were coming by train, and my father would take our horses and the spring wagon to pick them up at the station," answered Mammi.

"I'd like to have a ride on a train," said Emma.

"Well, maybe your parents will take you on a trip to visit your second cousins in Pennsylvania sometime. But if you children don't quit interrupting me, I can't tell you the story."

"We'll keep quiet and listen," Rachel declared. "Go on, Mammi."

"Anyway," Grandma began once more, "my mom knew Aunt Polly was used to having things just so. During the summer my parents lived in the summer kitchen, attached to the back of the house. There was more room there for canning fruits and vegetables. They only slept in the big house. Our good furniture and dishes were kept in the big house, too. In the fall when it got colder, we moved back into the big house.

"When Mother knew Aunt Polly was coming, she cleaned the big house, especially the living room. She warned all of us to stay out of the big house and not even open the living room door.

"She was busy the rest of the week. Saturday came and with it the visitors from Indiana. Mother had just finished baking bread, but she still had some pies in the oven. She went out to welcome her guests, and within herself she thought how nice

72

that the big house was clean and cool.

"Mother invited them in and took them to the door of the big house, through that kitchen, and into the living room. Ach, my! What a shock she had when she opened that door. Her nice clean, cool living room had chicken feathers scattered all over. How could such a thing have happened? She was so ashamed.

" 'Just sit here in the kitchen,' she told her company, 'until I get this mess cleaned up.' Of all people, Aunt Polly would have to be the one to come upon something like this.

"Three of the children had disobeyed the orders to stay out of the big house. We had some young roosters who were just beginning to crow. The children caught some of them and took them into the living room to teach them to crow right. They had looked carefully to make sure no one saw them sneak into the house. It was much cooler inside, out of the sun.

"The roosters, however, liked to be outside and flapped and struggled to be free. Mother found the children by the back porch, each holding a rooster. My brother Roy was saying, 'Rooster, now you *greh* (crow).' "

"Is this a true story, Grandma?" asked Rachel.

"Yes, I'm afraid so. We children were naughty and disobeyed."

"Someone saw the children go into that living room, even if your mother didn't," stated Rachel.

"Who?" asked Mary.

"Why, God did. My mom told me if we start to

do something we know is wrong and think no one sees us, we should look up into the sky. Maybe no one is on our left or right or anywhere in sight that we can see, but don't forget to look up," Rachel explained.

"That is true and good counsel," affirmed Grandma, pleased that Rachel taught the lesson this time.

"Anyway," Rachel continued, "I would let those young roosters learn to crow by themselves."

The invitation to Grandma and Grandpa's house was still open, and that night all of Roy's came for singing. It thrilled Rachel's heart to sense the kinship and unity of the large family group.

She couldn't help too well yet with the German songs, but she was determined to learn. Though the songs were sung slowly, there was a sweet, lofty melody that made her want to be able to understand the words. She would learn German. She vowed she would.

12

An Indian Remedy

When school began, Rachel moved back with her parents. Occasionally she was permitted to spend the weekend with her grandparents, Ellie and David. On one of those rare weekends, Rachel attended Amish church with Roy's family.

Scott and Mervin did not take too kindly to the idea, but her cousins Emma and Mary were excited. What fun they had sharing girl-talk and telling each other of their dreams for the future!

"I'm never getting married," Rachel once told her cousins.

"Why not?" asked Emma.

"I'd like to live in my own house and have a pretty flower garden and travel if I wanted to."

"That is just what I would like," agreed Mary.

"I have an idea, Mary," Rachel told her. "We could live together. Wouldn't that be fun?"

"Everybody would call you old maids then," Emma warned.

"Let them," remarked Rachel. "That wouldn't bother me."

"You are only twelve and could change your mind," Emma reminded Rachel.

"Wait and see," Rachel answered.

"But I thought you loved little babies so. Don't you ever want your own *schnuck Bupplin* (cute babies)?" Emma asked.

"Well, not right away. Maybe some day."

"See, you're already changing your mind," said Emma, laughing.

"You know," Rachel said wistfully, "I wish I could get Mammi to make me a new Amish cape dress and a pleated covering of my own. I hate to always ask to borrow from you."

"Oh, we don't mind. Do we Emma?" Mary said.

"Of course not, but I'm sure Grandma would be glad to make you a new outfit if you would ask her."

"Tell me, how do your parents feel about you wanting to be Amish?" Emma inquired.

"They don't seem to care, but Susie and Timothy say they can't understand me. Sometimes they call me *kleines* Amish *Meedel* (little Amish girl) or Black Stockings. They like all of you and seem to be glad when we come to visit. But they say they wouldn't want to dress so plain or do without a car, telephone, or electricity.

"I'm different. I like the way you live, and I think my mom does, too. Sometimes she talks about her growing-up years, and I believe she misses those times."

"Your folks were Amish once before they married and went to Central America."

"I know," answered Rachel.

"Do you think they will ever come back to the church?" Emma asked.

"If Mom would say she wants to, I believe they would. Dad would do a lot to make her happy. He loves her so, and she is a good mom."

This was rather strange for the cousins to hear Rachel speak so openly about her father's love for his wife. They weren't used to having much open affection expressed or shown. Like other Amish, they lived in respect and consideration for one another, and just knew love was there because of the caring actions.

That Saturday evening the girls were together on Roy's front porch.

"What are the boys doing across the road in the ditch?" asked Mary, looking down the lane.

"They seem to be hunting for something," observed Emma.

"Let's go see if we can help them," Rachel suggested.

The girls weren't aware that this is exactly what the boys wanted. Earlier they put their heads together in hopes of devising a plan to discourage Rachel from coming to visit and tagging along.

"Good! Our plan is starting to work already," chuckled Scott, as they saw the girls approaching.

"Yeah, and look who is the leader again," Mervin pointed out.

"Tagalong Rachel, naturally!"

"Hi," said Rachel. "What are you looking for?"

"Not for tagalongs, that's for sure," remarked Scott.

"Every time you come, Rachel, you girls have to go everywhere we go. We are going to call you Tagalong Rachel," complained Mervin.

"Don't be such a smart mouth," scolded Emma, "or I'll go tell Dad."

"All right then, if you must know, we were looking at this ivy here, with leaves in threes. Some people say it's poison, and if you get it on your skin, you break out with a bad itchy rash. But the Indians say if you eat a leaf you'll never get it. Rachel, don't you want to eat some?"

"Don't do it, Rachel," cried Emma and Mary, almost in the same breath.

"Sure, we figured she'd be too chicken to try it," scoffed Scott. "Sissy, sissy, tagalong!"

"I'm not chicken, and I'm not a sissy," Rachel told them.

"Oh, no? Well, then, why don't you eat some?" challenged Mervin.

"We dare you. Prove it. We double dare you!"

That was all it took for Rachel to grab a leaf from the bitter-tasting vine and pop it into her mouth.

"Oh, Rachel," exclaimed Mary. It was hard to swallow, but Rachel was too spunky to give up now.

"So there!" she crowed, once the foul-tasting leaf had disappeared down her throat. "That ought to show you I'm not a sissy."

The boys looked knowingly at each other. They

figured the worst was yet to come, and they were right. Several times that night Emma and Mary asked Rachel if she felt all right.

"I'm fine," she replied, and she never felt better.

Next morning the boys kept looking at Rachel in amazement. They fully expected her to be at least sick enough to go home. To their surprise, she was chipper as a canary. Maybe she hadn't eaten enough to do any harm.

The family all attended church, and Rachel went with them. She listened intently to the hymns and watched the solemn ministers file to their places. After the first minister spoke, they all knelt for prayer.

Then it happened. Suddenly Rachel felt very sick. She was hot, then cold, and then her cheeks filled with the bitter taste of the poison ivy leaf she had eaten.

Rachel knew she must leave the room, but one never left during prayer. She had no choice. Stumbling across the feet of the kneeling congregation, she barely made it outside. What bitter green liquid she brought up! She leaned against the porch railing for support.

Grandma Eash had seen her through a window as she arose from prayer, and with concern she made her way outdoors. "Rachel, what is wrong? Why, you are as white as a sheet! This green stuff smells so awful. What did you eat?"

"They told me to," Rachel gasped.

Grandma led her to a bench under one of the shade trees. By then Emma and Mary, who had been sitting next to Rachel in the house, joined them.

"Oh, Rachel, don't die," begged Mary nervously.

"Do you girls know anything about this?" asked Mommy.

"Mervin and Scott dared Rachel to eat poison ivy last night out by the ditch. They told her the Indians say if you eat it you will never get it."

"Oh," wailed Mary, "she probably won't live to get it."

"*Schtobb sell* (stop that)! Don't talk that way. Oh, those boys! Rachel, you should never take a dare. It's the sissy that follows the crowd, but a real woman or man stands alone. Well, we must get you home. Emma, go tell Grandpa to come out."

By the next day Rachel felt somewhat better, helped by home remedies. But it was more than a week until she was completely back to normal.

The boys knew they were in for punishment. Before it was administered by strap, they received it in a more drawn-out and miserable form. Both of them broke out with severe cases of poison ivy rash on their ankles, hands, and faces.

The experience did, however, break Rachel's habit of tagging along—at least she didn't do it as often.

13
Enough Pineapple

After that school year, Rachel got her parents' permission to stay with her Eash grandparents for another summer.

"Mammi," asked Rachel at the breakfast table one morning, "what are we going to do today?"

Every day seemed to hold surprisingly different things in store, and thirteen-year-old Rachel never knew what to expect. Some days if Roy's wife had canning to do, they would help her. Perhaps if it was a rainy day, Grandma Ellie would sit and mend for her daughter-in-law. It seemed like mending had a way of piling up fast for a large family such as Roy's.

"Well, today," replied Grandma, "I think we'll clean the basement and check the shelves to see how many jars of fruits and vegetables I have. That way I'll have an idea of how many I need to put up for the winter."

"You are the cleanest woman I ever saw," declared Grandpa. "I'm sure every shelf and jar will need to be washed and clean paper put down if you have your way."

"I'm glad my grandma isn't *schlappich* (sloppy)," commented Rachel.

"Oh, that's one thing she will never be," laughed Dawdy.

"Anyway, Mammi," volunteered Rachel, "I can help you count them. That's one thing I'm good at in school—arithmetic."

"You can help and so can Dawdy," answered Grandma.

"I've got other plans," Grandpa informed his wife.

"What plans?" asked Mammi.

"Well, I'll think of something if the ones I have aren't good enough," he replied.

Rachel knew Dawdy was only teasing by the twinkle in his eyes and the grin on his face. Grandma just laughed and said she suggests he change his plans.

That's how it came about that the three of them made their way down the narrow cellar steps, carrying old rags, buckets of water, a broom, and plenty of clean newspapers.

"Why do you have to wipe the jars?" asked Rachel. "The food on the inside can't get dirty."

"No," answered Mammi, "but the lids get so dusty and so do the jars. When we open them, we want them to be clean enough so no dust gets into the food."

"Couldn't we do that as we bring up a jar at a time to use?" Rachel wondered.

"She does that anyway," said Grandpa. "But you know Mammi. She can't stand dust. Maybe she never thought of it that we were made from dust, we fight it all our lives, and to dust we shall return."

To defend her Mammi, Rachel countered, "Well, Dawdy, would you want people to come down here and find things all *huddlich* (messy)?"

"Who would come down in our basement, anyway?" asked Dawdy.

"You never know," Mammi answered. "Let's get busy now. Dawdy, you can reach those jars on the top shelf for us. They are the hardest to get. Rachel, I'll wipe the jars and you count them. Put them over on the table underneath the small window until we get the shelf cleaned and fresh paper laid down. Then you give them to Dawdy, and he can put them back in place again." Grandma was a good organizer.

They worked busily, and Grandpa began to sing. It was a song Rachel especially liked. She had learned most of it, even though it was in German. The song was "Gott ist die Liebe (God is love)."

She loved Dawdy's deep strong voice and was just about to sing along when she let out a scream and dropped the jar Mammi handed her. The jar fell to the concrete floor and splintered into many slivers. Glass and pineapple lay at Rachel's feet, and she stood with both hands covering her face and trembling with fright.

"*Was ist letz* (what is wrong)?" asked her grandma anxiously.

"A spider," gasped Rachel, "a big ugly black spider."

"Where?" asked Grandpa.

"It was on my dress, but I don't know where it is now," answered the frightened girl.

"No doubt it is as far away as it can go, after that scream," laughed Dawdy.

"Don't tease her," said Mammi. "I never could stand those creepy things either."

"How well I remember," remarked Grandpa.

Rachel was crying now, partly from her scare and partly because of the broken jar. "Oh, Mammi, I'm so sorry. I've wasted a whole quart of pineapple and broken your jar," Rachel sobbed.

"Never mind. It's just one jar of fruit. We have plenty, and besides, it was an accident," Mammi comforted her.

Rachel would have felt better, though, if Dawdy had found that old spider and gotten rid of it for good.

"You know," mused Grandpa, "this pineapple was ruined through a scare you had. Ask your grandmother about another jar of pineapple that was wasted."

"Ach, Dawdy, you would bring that up!" responded Mammi.

Sensing that a story might be forthcoming, Rachel fished for it. "What does he mean, Mammi?"

"Let's just get our work finished down here. Then perhaps tonight I'll tell you."

That satisfied Rachel. She worked diligently, watching for any spiders hiding in the dark corners of the cellar.

"There it is!" screeched Rachel, quickly jumping on the steps leading out of the basement.

"There what is?" asked Grandpa.

"The spider! Right over by the drain," answered Rachel. Grandpa saw it and quickly did away with the intruder. Now Rachel felt so much better. Nevertheless, she was happiest once every jar had been cleaned, counted, and replaced, and they were out of the cellar.

That evening after supper, as Rachel and Grandma were doing the dishes, Rachel brought up the subject of the wasted pineapple Grandpa had mentioned earlier.

"Rachel," began Grandma, "some people don't believe in telling about things they did while growing up, especially if they were naughty. But I think you can learn from our mistakes, and thus I can teach you."

"Yes, Grandma," answered Rachel, "and I want to learn what is right."

"Well, I love pineapple," said Mammi. "It's my favorite fruit. My mother used to can pineapple, but since we were a large family, I never seemed to get enough of it.

"One day a naughty plan popped into my head when I was sent to the basement for something. I decided that when mother would lie down with the baby for a nap, I would take a spoon, open a quart of pineapple, and eat it all by myself.

"I made sure none of my brothers or sisters saw me go to the basement. I opened a jar and ate as fast as I could. When I had eaten half of the contents, I was full.

"So I placed the now half-empty jar back on the shelf. I decided to come back another day and eat the rest of the pineapple. But, ach, my! I forgot about it until . . . one day Mother had me help her in the basement just as we did today. Suddenly I heard her ask, '*Was ist des* (what is this)?'

"As I turned, I saw her holding a half-empty jar of green, moldy pineapple. I'm sure guilt was written all over my face, because she said, 'Ellie, what do you know about this?' "

"Oh, Mammi, what did you do?" asked Rachel.

"I told the truth!"

"Then what happened?"

"I would rather have taken the *Bletsching* (spanking) we most always got. What I had to do was much harder for me. I had to take that smelly jar of pineapple, show it to all the family, and tell them what I had done."

"Were you ashamed?" asked Rachel.

"I certainly was. My papa was pretty strict, and I didn't know what he might do. I had to wash the dishes by myself that night, and there were stacks of them. It was hard to clean that jar. For a long time, I couldn't eat pineapple."

"But you like it now, don't you?" asked Rachel.

"Oh, yes," answered Grandma.

"But only a dessert dish full at a time," laughed Dawdy, who had been listening from his place in the living room.

Rachel joined in the merriment, and everything seemed all right with the world again.

14
A Falling Saucer

By the time Rachel was fourteen years old, she had become good friends with some of the Amish girls who were about her age. "Mom," she asked her mother one Sunday in the early fall, "the next time I am allowed to go to Amish church with Roy's or Dawdy's, may I invite some of my Amish girlfriends to our house?"

"Yes, I think that would be nice, but I'm not sure if they would be allowed to come."

"Why wouldn't they be?" asked Rachel.

"Some of their parents may feel we are trying to lure them away from their belief."

"Oh, no, Mom," exclaimed Rachel, "I want them just to visit. Besides, they know I'm going to be Amish when I'm grown."

"Rachel, we don't know what the future holds for us. Perhaps you will embrace the Amish way of life, but you are still so young and could change your mind yet."

"No, I won't," she insisted. "Anyway, could I ask my friends to come?"

"You may ask them, but don't be too disappointed if some of them say no."

Rachel's friends were pleased when she invited them.

"Go ask your parents right away," she urged them, after they had eaten their church meal.

Each case was the same. Every mother had to consult with her husband, whom she regarded as the head of the household. As a good Amish wife, she would hardly make such a decision without talking it over with her spouse.

Therefore, it took some time before each girl could report back to Rachel. She was shocked, for each answer was the same. They were allowed to come if it would be at Roy's house or Grandpa and Grandma's, but they would rather not have them visit Rachel's home.

Rachel did not understand. Well, she would just ask Grandma whether she could have her friends at their place if she would help with the meal.

Grandma was more than willing and began to help Rachel make plans right away. "We can have it on one of our between Sundays, Rachel," she offered.

"Mom said maybe it's too much to ask of you," reported Rachel.

"No, it isn't at all," Mammi assured her. "Now what do you think we should plan for the meal?"

"Oh, I thought I could bring some of our canned beef, and peas, applesauce, and—"

That's as far as she got when Grandma interrupted: "Whoa, Rachel, I want to furnish some things. Let me make potatoes, gravy, cracker pudding, and cake or pie."

"I want to make dessert, Mammi. Besides, you shouldn't fix anything. It's my company."

"But I want to help," insisted Grandma Ellie. "It will be so much fun to have young girls visiting again. How many will be coming?"

"Four, as far as I know. Of course, that's not counting Roy's girls. I want Emma and Mary to come."

"I thought you would. They always liven things up, and I like it when they come over."

The special Sunday finally arrived. Mammi and Rachel had things well in hand and were eagerly watching for the guests. Soon they saw Sam Erb's girls come up their drive. Grandpa went out to unhitch for them and led the horse to a stall in the barn.

Gertie and Ada made their way to the house, where Rachel met them and took their bonnets. It was warm enough that shawls or short black coats which they usually wore weren't necessary.

After shaking hands with Grandma, Gertie asked, "Aren't the others here yet?"

"Not yet," replied Rachel. "Oh, here are Mary and Emma. Come in," she said, opening the screen door. "Gertie and Ada just got here."

"Yes, we saw them drive in."

"My, something smells *wunderbaar* (wonderful) good," Ada commented.

"Well, let's go on in the living room, and when Viola and Cora get here, we will eat." Rachel led them through the kitchen.

They made their way to the living room and talked about the new summer dresses they were getting, how Lefs Raymond's little Mosie fell in the watering trough and almost drowned, and other woman-talk.

"Here come Cora and Viola now," announced Rachel. "Good, everyone is here."

Dawdy went to take care of their horse, too, but this time Roy's William offered to see to it. Rumors were that William had his eye on Viola, but he denied it.

"Come in, girls," invited Rachel. She took their bonnets and then ushered them into the living room, where they made sure they shook hands with each one.

"We didn't keep you waiting, did we?" asked Cora.

"Not really," answered Rachel, "but I guess we can get the food on now."

"We'll help you," volunteered all six girls. With that many willing hands, they were soon seated at the table. They bowed their heads in silent prayer. Rachel's Dad prayed aloud at mealtime and during family devotions. That was all right, but somehow Rachel preferred to pray her own silent prayer.

After the delicious meal, the girls did the dishes and cleaned up the kitchen. They sang a few choruses as they worked. When everything was cleared away, they sat out on the porch with the

German songbook and a hymnal with English songs.

Asking Grandma and Grandpa to join them, they sang heartily. They loved to sing, as do most Amish. They knew that many of their hymns were written during a time of great persecution for their forbears. Thus, the hymns have deep and reverent meaning.

By and by, the girls were thirsty. "Let's go inside and get a drink," suggested Rachel. "My throat is dry after all that singing."

"Mine, too," said Gertie.

A day with other youth would not be complete without a bit of a joke, Viola thought. "Say," she remarked to Rachel, "did you know that you can pin a saucer to the ceiling?"

"Oh no, you can't!" answered Rachel.

"You just get an old saucer, put some water in it, bring me a broom, and I'll show you," Viola told Rachel.

"I still don't believe it, but I'll see what you claim you can do." Rachel went to get a saucer, water, and the broom. When she came back, Cora had moved a chair to the center of the room. Grandma and Grandpa stood nearby, watching this but saying not a word. Grandpa had a bit of a grin on his face, and Rachel figured he doubted Viola, too.

Viola took the saucer which contained water and climbed up on the chair. "Now, Rachel, place the broom handle firmly against the center of the saucer."

Rachel did as she was told while Viola removed a

91

pin from her head covering and proceeded to try to stick it through the saucer into the ceiling. Then she dropped the pin. Emma and Ada began to hunt for it, but said they couldn't see it anywhere. Rachel suggested they give Viola another pin.

"We can't do that," Viola informed Rachel. "It has to be this certain kind of pin."

Viola came down from the chair and began to look around as though searching for the pin. Naturally, Rachel couldn't help them look; she had to keep her eyes on the saucer. The next thing she knew, the girls put the chair back in its place at the table.

All of them began to laugh as Gertie commented, "Looks like you will have to stand there all day or figure out a way to get that dish down from there. It might be a flying saucer."

Rachel joined in the laughter when she realized the joke was on her. It was an old Amish trick, and she had fallen for it. She jumped back, let the saucer fall, and caught it so it wouldn't break. Some of the water *schpritzed* (splashed) on her, and the girls cheered. As she got the mop to clean up the wet spot on the floor, she asked, "Dawdy, did you know about this?"

"Oh, I've seen it played on someone several times, but I wasn't going to spoil the fun."

"I'll just have to remember not to fall for things I can hardly believe in the first place," Rachel mused. "But we are still all friends, and it's been a good day."

So it was.

15
Mistaken Identity

It was unusual for Amish children to accompany their parents to the large city. There were too many worldly things there for them to see. Therefore, fifteen-year-old Rachel listened intently as Grandma told her about one such trip her parents made when she was a little girl.

"My mother and father did not go to the big city of Columbus often, and we children even less. Actually, I can remember only one time when I was allowed to go, and that was for a specialist to check my ears. I had a lot of earaches as a child."

"Why weren't you allowed to go along to the city?" asked Rachel.

"My dad didn't believe in spending money unless it was absolutely necessary. We had to drive about five miles to Plumwood, where we boarded a trolley—"

"What's a trolley?" Rachel interrupted.

"It's a streetcar that runs on tracks."

"Oh, you mean like a train," volunteered Rachel.

"Something like that, only it didn't travel fast, and it went down the middle of the street. It often stopped for people to get on and off.

"I remember that we left our horse and buggy at the livery stable, where a man took care of it for twenty-five cents. He put it in a shed with other horses and saw to it that they had hay, grain, and water.

"It cost a quarter each to ride the trolley and a nickel extra for each child. Papa said it cost too much to take us children unless there was a good reason."

"Did you like the big city when you got to go along that one time?"

"Rachel, I felt almost guilty when Papa slowly took the nickel from his pocket to pay my fare. And then the huge buildings were such a surprise to me. And there were people everywhere. I wondered if we could find our way back home again, ever!

"We went straight to the doctor's office, and I stayed close to my mother. We rode in an elevator up to the seventh floor. It gave me a funny feeling in my stomach. Papa told me I'd better not get sick, so I tried hard not to."

"What did the doctor do to your ears?" Rachel asked.

"He looked inside them with a little flashlight. Then he put some drops in one ear and gave us a prescription to get some drops to take home. I saw

Papa frown and I felt guilty again. I wished my ears didn't hurt and I wouldn't be so much trouble. I did not want Papa to have to spend money for me."

"Was your papa poor?" asked Rachel.

"Ach, my, no. He was never poor, but he just believed in being thrifty."

"What happened when you left the doctor's office?"

"We wanted to do a little shopping at a five-and-ten store. On our way I saw the prettiest glass bowl in a window. There was a little wooden boy and girl in the bowl, and they were skating. Music came from it, and snow was falling as the bowl turned slowly around and around. I had never seen anything so lovely, Rachel."

"Oh Mammi, I know what that was. It must have been a music box!"

"Yes, that's what it was," answered Grandma.

"Did they buy it for you?" Rachel wondered.

"No, it was considered a worldly thing."

"Why does everything that's pretty seem to be worldly?" asked Rachel.

"Well, let me finish my story first," answered Grandma. "I was so fascinated by the pretty sight that I stopped to gaze at it in wonder. Realizing someone was standing by my side, I gave a tug at the dress and said, 'Oh, Mom, can I have it?'

"The lady standing next to me began laughing. 'You really like that music box, don't you?' she asked.

"I stood there speechless and afraid. I had thought the lady beside me was my mother."

"Where was your mother?" inquired Rachel.

"They hadn't noticed that I lagged behind, and they were down the street a ways."

"Did they come back and get you?"

"Of course they did, and I was so glad to see them. The lady whom I had mistaken as my mom smiled and told my parents that it would make me happy if I could have that music box.

"Dad said 'Humph' as he took my hand and pulled me away from the window. But as we walked on, he told me music is the way of the world, and such things are *Augenlust* (lust of the eyes, 1 John 2:16) and not for our people."

"Grandma, are you happy being Amish?" asked Rachel.

"Yes, I am. I would have it no other way."

"Were you sad that you couldn't have the music box and that you made a mistake because you didn't know your mother wasn't there with you?"

"I was only too glad to be back with my mom and dad. But, Rachel, I made a bigger mistake years later in somewhat the same way."

"Tell me about it," begged Rachel.

"Grandpa and I often laugh about it now, but at the time it wasn't funny. We had been to a wedding and, since it was of a close friend of ours, we were invited to stay for supper. By the time we were ready to go home, it was dark.

"Grandpa came to the kitchen where I was visiting with other women and announced that he would get the rig and pick me up at the front gate. Other people were also leaving, so Katie Hershberger and I both made our way to the washhouse for our shawls. Then we went out to wait for our rides home.

"There was the buggy already waiting at the front gate. I said good-bye to Katie and climbed into the buggy. We left and drove about a half mile before it appeared to me that something wasn't quite right.

" 'David,' I said, 'this isn't our horse!'

" 'Yes,' a voice responded, 'and you are not my wife, either.'

"You see, Rachel, our buggies have such dim lamps that I didn't notice it was not my husband sitting in that buggy. Neither did the driver detect that I was not his wife. I hadn't paid attention to the horse. Many horses and all our buggies looked so much alike."

"What did you do when you noticed?" Rachel asked with a chuckle.

"We turned around in a hurry and went back to where some bewildered people were waiting. So that makes two times that I made the wrong identification."

"Well, Mammi, it can happen to anyone. At our church once," shared Rachel, "I thought Simon Lapp was my dad. I pulled his coattail and asked if he had any more wintergreen candy, and could I have some. Oh, I was so ashamed when I knew what I had done.

"He was real nice about it, though, and said I needn't be ashamed. Then he put his hand into his coat pocket and asked me if peppermint would do instead. I didn't want to accept it, but he insisted and assured me that he knew I was a good girl.

"When I told my parents, they said I must learn to look before I leap. At that time I did not know what they meant, but since I'm older I do.

"Mammi, if you were allowed to have a music box, I'd buy you one once I'd have enough money. They have some real nice ones at Heffner's store."

"That's nice of you, Rachel, but the only music I want is the sound of my children and grandchildren, singing the dear old hymns when we all get together. There is no music sweeter than that."

"But you can't see the little boy and girl skating in the snow," remarked Rachel.

"Oh yes, I can. How many times have Dawdy and I watched our grandchildren skate on the pond? Yes, even in the snow."

"Mammi, you are so content and it takes so little to make you and Dawdy happy. Some day I want to live just as you do," Rachel told her.

"Nothing would make us happier," answered Mammi.

"Then I shall," Rachel resolved.

16
A Church Shower

Rachel heard the menfolk laughing and talking as they were visiting underneath the maple tree. So, naturally, she made her way to the front yard. Today was Ascension Day, which all Amish and some other Christians observe as a holiday. James and Rebecca had invited both sets of grandparents and the families of Sam and Eli for lunch.

The meal was finished, and the men had made themselves comfortable to visit a while. Women's work was to do the dishes and tend the babies. Rachel had helped until she and her cousins were told they were free for the afternoon. The girls went down to the pond, a favorite spot, and settled down to catch up on all the news.

"Do you know," said Rachel, "I heard that John Dannie's Lizabet is going to start her *Rumschpringe* (running around with young folk) any time now."

"She just turned sixteen, and around that age the

Amish are allowed to *schpringe rum* with the singing bunch," Orpha told her.

"I'm almost sixteen," Rachel informed them.

"Is it true that you want to be Amish like us?" Mattie asked.

"Yes, it is," Rachel confirmed.

She noticed the girls looking at each other with strange expressions.

"What's wrong with that? Why are you looking so *schpottich* (mockingly) at me?"

"You are used to all the worldly things. Your folks have electricity and a phone, and, of course, a car. We don't think you would want to give all that up. It's different living without them once you had them," Elsie explained. The other girls all agreed.

"I've spent my summers with Mammi and Dawdy Eash since I was twelve, and before that I was often there a few days at a time. They don't have those modern things. I enjoyed my time with them," Rachel responded.

"Yes, but you know you can go back to your parents any time you get tired of doing without modern stuff," countered Mattie.

"Ach, I won't get tired of it at all." Rachel used *ach* to show her cousins how well she handled Amish words. "It's fun to ride in a buggy. Dawdy lets me have the reins and drive by myself sometimes.

"When you don't have electric, then you don't have to worry when the power goes off. As far as a telephone goes, if you do without, you don't have a bill to pay. In an emergency, I could use a neighbor's phone or a public one out by the roadside."

"Even if you would go Amish, it probably wouldn't last because your mom and dad didn't," Elsie reminded her.

"But that was because my dad felt a call to go to Central America," Rachel replied.

"They are back now, so why didn't they join the Amish again?" Orpha remarked.

"Sometimes I think my mom would like to, and maybe some day they will," Rachel answered.

"We doubt that," murmured Elsie, and the girls snickered again.

Just then the boys came to the pond. Rachel was glad, for she didn't like the tone the conversation was taking.

"Hey," shouted Mosie, "want to play Lose Your Supper?"

"Sure," answered all four girls.

With eight boys (including the smaller ones) and four girls holding hands, it made a nice circle. Two youths clasped hands and ran around the outside of the ring. They would tap where the hands of two players joined and keep running.

The tapped pair had to run together around the circle the opposite way, trying to reach the vacant spot first. The first pair there joined hands with the circle. Whichever couple got there last was said to lose their supper. They ran on and tapped another couple.

Partners were not permitted to unclasp hands while running together. Some of the younger ones couldn't keep up, so they were almost dragged. Finally, one of Eli's boys picked up his partner, little

Davy, and carried him. Everyone giggled at this sight.

When they grew tired of this game, they played Three Deep. Rachel heard the grown-ups laughing and wished she could join them. She did not have long to wait. While running, Mosie fell and bumped his nose hard, so they took him to the house to stop the bleeding.

"My, you children look worn out," observed Grandma Miller. "Maybe you had better sit here with us and rest awhile. Yost, you are so sweaty, it looks as if your hair has just been washed."

This was what Rachel had been waiting to hear, an invitation to join the grown-ups. The babies were taking naps, and Grandpa Miller said he could stand one, too.

It was so much fun to sit and listen to older people talk. All the young folks plopped down on the soft, sweet-smelling grass. Rachel found her place closest to both her grandmas. Rebecca had popped some popcorn and brought bowls for each one, along with apples and a large pitcher of lemonade.

"I don't see how anyone can eat another bite," teased Grandma Miller. "You had such a delicious dinner."

"Well, it's here for those who want some," offered Rebecca. The children had worked up hearty appetites after their games. Mosie soon joined them, feeling fine.

"Just don't you children take more than you can eat or drink," James advised them. "I'm convinced we often overeat and that, too, is called sin. Our wives are good cooks, but after seeing how little the people in Central America had compared with our abundance, I'm more aware of our wastefulness."

"I agree with you, James," affirmed Grandpa. "Gluttony is surely wrong. We need to be more thankful and share that which we have been blessed with."

"Eli, don't fill your glass so full of lemonade or we may have another church shower," someone called out, and the men began to laugh. Now Rachel was about to hear the story she had missed earlier.

"What do you mean by that?" asked Eli.

"I'll let your grandpa tell you," his dad answered.

"Sometimes, as you know," began Grandpa, "church is held at a farm where there is a small house. When the weather is nice, services may be conducted in a shed or even on the barn floor between haymows.

"A number of years ago there was a man in our group who was rather ill-tempered. One day during church services he had taken one of his young sons out to *bletsche* (spank) him for not sitting quietly during preaching.

"It so happened that at the same time his wife took their little daughter for a drink from the water pail by the barn entrance. After the little one drank deeply from the common dipper, there was still some water left. Not knowing what else to do with the leftover water, she gave it a fling out the entranceway.

103

"At that very moment, her disgruntled husband came around the corner with his subdued little boy in tow. The water hit her husband smack in the face. He began to sputter, and she quickly made her way back to her seat. People called it a real church shower."

"What did the man do to his wife?" asked Rachel, while everyone roared.

"I don't know," answered Grandpa. "But if I know your grandma, she could make a lesson even from this."

"Just be glad it wasn't you who got showered, Dawdy," Mammi responded. "It was an accident, I'm sure, and he probably forgave his wife. If that would have happened to us, Dawdy," she added, "we would have laughed all the way home." And Rachel knew that was true.

The rest of the day was pleasantly spent in more visiting and the usual singing. When the babies woke from their naps, Rachel enjoyed feeding one of the *schnuck Bupplin* (cute babies).

As Sam's left, Elsie called out to Rachel, "Goodbye, almost-Amish girl."

Rachel didn't know whether she was poking fun at her or if she approved of her desire to become Amish. But she wasn't going to let it spoil her day. Tonight she would just savor the good time they had shared together.

17
Thou Shalt Not Steal

Grandma was always teaching her grandchildren worthwhile verses. Dawdy, too, was concerned that they grow up in the nurture and admonition of the Lord, as the Bible teaches. They felt that just because their own family was grown and married, their responsibility and opportunity did not end there.

One German verse often repeated went like this:

Kind, lass allein
was nicht ist dein.
(Child, leave alone
What you don't own.)

"Rachel, never take anything which isn't yours."

"Ach, Mammi, I wouldn't unless someone wanted to give me something," Rachel answered.

"That's different. Of course, you would take it, for it would be a gift. I'm thinking of two boys who were tempted to take something once. Not only were they tempted, they took it and paid dearly later."

"Tell me about it, Mammi, please do," Rachel begged. Even though she was nearly sixteen now, she still loved to hear stories from the past and the lessons they taught.

"Maybe I'd better ask Dawdy first," answered Grandma Ellie.

"Why must you ask him? He tells me stories, too, and sometimes they are about things which happened in your growing-up years."

"You see, Rachel, one of those boys who got into trouble was Dawdy. He may not care for you to know how mischievous he used to be."

"He wouldn't care if I knew. All little boys are rowdy at times."

"Just the same, it may be better if I ask him," said Grandma.

"How soon? Will you ask him when he comes in at lunchtime?" asked Rachel.

"If I don't forget," Mammi answered.

"I won't let you forget," Rachel assured her. Grandma knew she wouldn't.

Grandpa often helped with lighter work, such as driving horses during haying time or running the binder to cut oats or wheat.

"Why does Dawdy have to work? He's getting old. Couldn't he just stay in the house or help us in the garden?" Rachel reasoned.

"It's good for us older people to keep busy if we are able. If we just sit around all the time, our joints will grow stiff and soon we couldn't work at all.

"Besides, we are happier if we can help out and know we are still needed. Dawdy always did like the outdoors, to work the soil, watch things grow, and reap a harvest. He will always be a farmer at heart."

"And I'll always need you and Dawdy," Rachel assured her grandmother. "We all do, and it just wouldn't be the same without you."

Grandma just smiled, but it thrilled her heart to hear her granddaughter say so.

"I'm going down the lane to get the mail, Mammi."

Rachel was walking in her bare feet, kicking up little clouds of dust with each step. The wild roses were in bloom, and she decided to pick a few to carry back for Grandma to enjoy. She lay the weekly Amish newspaper called *The Budget* and a few letters beside the lane and stepped into the grass to gather the roses.

Suddenly her foot hurt something terrible. Forgetting the flowers, she gathered up the mail and hobbled to the house.

Her cousin Mary saw her limping and called out, "Rachel, what's wrong?"

Rachel was too close to crying to answer. She just waved and made her way to the *Dawdy Haus*.

"*Was ist letz* (what is wrong)?" asked Grandma, seeing her dilemma.

"Something stung my foot," Rachel whimpered, lifting it for Grandma to take a look.

"Ach, my, a honeybee stung you. He left his stinger, too. Come now, sit here on the woodbox, and I'll take it out." The woodbox was near the stove and looked almost like a cedar chest in size, but was painted a dull red. It was a favorite place for boys and girls to sit.

Rachel sat and raised her throbbing foot for Grandma's soothing care. It hurt even after Grandma removed the stinger and treated it with a pasty mixture of baking soda and water.

"Mammi, I have heard that some people are allergic to bee stings, and some have died because of them," Rachel fearfully told her.

"Yes, it has happened, but it's quite uncommon."

"I'm wearing my shoes outside after this!" vowed Rachel. "It still hurts so *wunderbaar* (terribly)."

"Would you like to hear the story now that I mentioned earlier about the two naughty boys? Maybe Dawdy wouldn't care if I told you, and it might help you forget the pain."

Rachel doubted it could do that, but she was ready to hear the story.

"When your grandpa was about eight years old, he and his brother were staying with their grandparents one day while their mother and father went to town. Grandpa asked one of them to bring him the nail clippers from the medicine cabinet.

"In that cabinet they spied a box of gum. Since they seldom had any gum, the temptation was too much. Slipping the whole box into his pocket, your grandpa waited until his brother obediently took the clippers to his Dawdy.

"Both boys then made their way to the barn. There they divided the gum and stuffed every piece in their mouths and chewed away. But the gum they took was no ordinary gum at all."

"What was it, Grandma?"

"Well, it was Feen-a-mint gum. It works the same as castor oil, and you know what that does to you."

"It must have tasted awful! How could they chew it?" remarked Rachel.

"The taste wasn't bad at all," answered Grandma Ellie, "but the result was more of a problem. They almost wore out the path going back and forth to the outhouse. It was a lesson they never forgot.

"Dawdy says that's when he first learned the verse, 'Kind, lass allein / was nicht ist dein.' "

"In the Ten Commandments that we learned in Sunday school, it says, 'Thou shalt not steal,' " Rachel told Mammi.

"Yes, that is one of God's commandments, and we must learn to obey it and not only say it."

Grandma was right: the story, and possibly the soda paste, helped Rachel forget how badly the sting hurt. At noon she asked Grandpa if he still liked Feen-a-mint gum.

"Ach, Mammi, you have been telling stories again. Rachel, remember, if we take small things that don't belong to us, soon we'll want more things of greater value. We can also steal time, and maybe even another person's good name."

"Oh, Dawdy, I don't want to steal anything, but if you want to give me gum, please make sure it's the ordinary kind."

"It just so happens that I have some spearmint gum right here in my pocket. Before I give it to you, repeat the little German verse again."

Rachel gladly obliged.

Feelings were beginning to stir within Rachel which troubled her at times. She loved her parents dearly and learned much from the teachings of the church they attended.

Yet somehow there was still something within her drawing her toward the way of the Amish. What should she do? Rachel wanted to do what was best for her.

At times her brothers and sister made her feel as if she were strange because she considered embracing the Amish belief and lifestyle. Rachel decided she would talk to Dawdy and Mammi about the matter. They were so wise.

But for now she would just enjoy the gum Dawdy had given her and curl up on the porch swing while Mammi took her afternoon nap. Yes, that's what she would do, she would ask her grandparents' advice. They would not make fun of her. She loved their way of teaching. Rachel was sure they could help.

18
High-Button Shoes

"Mammi," Rachel asked her grandma one day, "what do you think I should do? I love my parents and the church where we go. Many of the young folks there are my friends, but I have friends in your church, too."

Grandma waited for her to continue, but when she didn't, Mammi encouraged her by reflecting her words. "Well then, I would say you have a lot of friends, and that is nice."

"But that isn't what I mean. I like my friends, but sometimes they make *Schpott* (fun) of me and mock at the fact that I'd like to become Amish. Mammi, what do you and Dawdy think I should do?"

"You must pray much about it, Rachel. It would make us happy indeed if you lived a plain and simple way of life."

"Can't my family live like that?" asked Rachel.

"Yes, they can, but it seems so often one step leads to another."

"You mean, soon people aren't satisfied and want more modern things?"

"That's exactly what I mean, Rachel."

"Our family doesn't want all the modern things the world has. My mom and dad live plainer than many in the church."

"That's true, Rachel, and Dawdy and I appreciate it, but look at your sister, Susan. I notice that she keeps fancying up her dresses more and more. Lately she's been parting her hair on the side. What will she want next?"

"Her boyfriend likes her fancy dresses. He told her, too, that she looks prettier with her hair parted on the side," responded Rachel.

"But what is her reason for doing these things? Is it to please herself and her boyfriend? I am sure your family studies the Bible and prays, but, oh, I know how Dawdy and I longed for your parents to stay within our own church."

"You know, Mom sometimes still makes remarks that show me she misses the Amish way."

Mammi's heart skipped a beat at this bit of information. Maybe, oh, just maybe, James and Rebecca would come back.

"The thing is, Grandma," Rachel continued, "I don't like when people make *Schpott* of me."

"But Rachel, they mocked Jesus when he walked this earth, and he took it all patiently. Besides, let them mock away, for sometimes their chickens will come home to roost."

Rachel wondered what chickens had to do with it, but she didn't need to wonder long.

"I'm going to tell you about just such a case. There was a poor widow woman who had a family of five children. Her oldest boy was nine. She struggled hard to keep her family fed and clothed.

"Then one day their house burned. The church moved a small building on the property for her and her five children. As time passed, this lady married a man with four children of his own. Now there were nine mouths to feed.

"Times were hard, for this was during the Great Depression."

"What's the Great Depression?" asked Rachel.

"That was when many people lost their life savings and even their homes. The banks went under, and work was hard to find.

"People who lived on farms were able to survive because at least they raised much of their own food, and had milk and eggs, and meat from butchering. But I'm getting away from my story about high-button shoes."

"What?" exclaimed Rachel, "I thought you were going to tell me about chickens. Now you mention high-button shoes!"

"Don't be impatient, Rachel. It all ties together. To help with expenses, this poor family kept several hives of bees. They sold honey in the comb, and people liked it."

"I wouldn't like honey in my comb," Rachel informed Mammi. "My hair would get all stuck together, and it's tangled enough."

"Ach, no, Rachel, not that kind of comb. The honey is in a little square wooden box with waxlike compartments. Once the honey was all gone, we loved to use the waxy part for chewing gum. Anyway, those were hard times."

"But weren't they called 'the good old days'?" interjected her granddaughter again.

"You could call it that. One good thing back then was that we learned to depend on God!" Grandma thought it would be easier to tell a story if Rachel didn't interrupt so often.

"I must tell you about Lucy Felch and her daughter Maria," Mammi continued. "One day after doing some shopping in town, Mrs. Felch decided to go by the place where that good comb honey was sold. She had heard so much about it.

"As they pulled into the Hershberger drive, Maria noticed a boy about her own age getting a drink of water from the outdoor pump. She could tell he had just come from hard work in the field, for his shirt was drenched with sweat.

"Maria had seen this boy at her school, but she never knew where he lived. It appeared as though he had outgrown his trousers, for his pant legs were short."

"That's what some school children call 'high waters,'" Rachel said.

"No matter," Mammi told her. "We shouldn't label anything like that. Maria remained seated on the buggy and held the reins while her mother made the purchase she came for.

"Leon, the boy, stared at Maria, and she stared back. Then Maria saw Leon was wearing girl's high-button shoes. This seemed strange and humorous to her. As Lucy Felch returned with her purchase and they drove out the lane, Maria began to laugh.

" 'What's so funny?' her mother asked.

" 'That boy,' she chuckled, 'he . . . ha, ha, ha, ha . . . he . . . ha, ha ha . . . he was wearing . . . ha, ha!'

" 'Would you stop laughing and tell me what boy and what he was wearing?' demanded Lucy.

" 'You know, Leon—the boy who was getting a drink at the pump. Well, his pant legs were way too short, and he . . . ha, ha, ha . . . was wearing . . . ha, ha . . . girls' high-button . . . ha, ha, ha . . . shoes!' Then Maria burst out in a fit of laughter.

" 'Maria, you ought to be ashamed,' her mother rebuked her. 'Don't you realize these people are poor? Likely enough those shoes were given to the family or maybe were hand-me-downs. The boy looked as though he had been working hard. Perhaps those shoes hurt his feet, since they were made for girls.'

"But Maria just laughed and mocked some more. Every once in a while she would say, 'Girls' high-button shoes, ha, ha, ha!'

"Finally, Lucy Felch declared, 'Maria, since you make *Schpott* of Leon, it would serve you right if some day you were to become his wife.' The idea brought more peals of laughter.

"But, you know, Rachel, that's exactly what happened years later."

"Did it really, Grandma?" asked Rachel with surprise.

"Yes, it did."

"Did Maria still make fun of Leon after they were married?"

"No, she didn't. But that's what I meant about chickens coming home to roost. The things we do or say sometimes come back to us."

"I'm glad Maria didn't mock him any more. It isn't pleasant when someone makes fun of you."

"Leon and Maria were never well-to-do financially, but they both had the finer things of life."

"What do you mean?" Rachel asked.

"The best things in life, my girl, are love, joy, peace, long-suffering, patience, temperance, meekness, and faith."

"Was Maria ever sorry she married Leon?"

"No, and although she was often teased, the only thing she regretted was making fun of him that summer day so long ago. Rachel, those who mock can only hurt us as much as we allow them to. The ones they really harm are themselves."

Once more Grandma Ellie had given her granddaughter food for thought. Even Rachel did not realize what a comfort and help that day's conversation would be in months to come.

19
I Took the Floor

That summer was fast drawing to a close, and Rachel would soon return home again. She looked forward to being with her parents, brothers, and sister, but she knew she would miss spending days with her grandparents. With her cousins right next door, there was always something interesting going on.

Scott and Mervin still called her Tagalong Rachel, but just in fun now. To be truthful, they rather enjoyed her company. She had a way of keeping things lively, and they had to admit she made a nice-looking Amish girl. With her parents' permission, they even took her along to the singing once, just after her sixteenth birthday.

Grandma Ellie had made her a complete Amish outfit for being such a big help to her over the past months. Rachel looked neat in her dark green dress, white cape, and apron. The white covering fit nicely on her head, but could not completely hide her dark wavy hair. She would fit in with the Amish girls, who wear black coverings to church, but white ones for Sunday night singings.

"I'm glad we're going to a singing and not a German spelling bee," Rachel told her cousins, as they drove along through the countryside in the family's two-seat buggy.

"Why do you say that?" asked Scott.

"Because I can sing German pretty good now, but I sure couldn't spell the words."

"I rather like the spellings. We have one every Wednesday night. Last week I almost got the floor," Mary informed her.

"Grandma told me once that she should have had the floor, but the prize went to another girl."

"Mammi is the storytellingest person I ever saw," remarked Mervin.

"There is no such word as *storytellingest*," protested Rachel. "She tells the best stories I've ever heard. They are true, and that makes them so much fun to listen to."

"Well, what did she tell you about the German spelling?" asked Scott. "I don't see how she finds time to tell so many stories. We always have to work."

"She tells them while we work," Rachel told them. "I'm going to move back home soon, so the other day Mammi decided she wanted me to help her clean out some drawers. Many old family treasures are kept in those places, and it sure was a fun time.

"Grandpa had gone to town, so Mammi said it would be a good time to straighten things, for Dawdy wouldn't be underfoot, as she put it. I asked her why it's so much more fun for me to work with her than at my house. She thought it was because there are older things to see at her house.

"Like the old German ABC spelling book. Its pages are all brown and worn. It had someone else's name in it, but that name was marked out and underneath was Grandma's name.

"I asked her if she could spell German. She said she used to. Everyone would line up on the floor, and whoever remained standing longest without missing a word took the floor."

"We know that, jabberbox," teased Scott. "Remember, we go to German spellings, too."

"If I don't tell it like Grandma did, it won't be the same," Rachel informed him.

"Let her talk," Mary insisted. "I want to hear what happened."

"Well, Mammi said we had to do our work right, so I laid the old book on the bed as we went on sorting and cleaning. Grandpa laughed at us later and said he doesn't suppose many things ended up in the wastebasket.

"Mammi told him she doesn't believe in wasting things. 'As the old adage goes,' she remembered, 'waste not, want not.' Grandpa just smiled. He knows Mammi is not wasteful. The only things I remember throwing away were a large rubber band, an old letter from a suds company, and a broken comb.

"Mammi saw that the drawers were neater, and she could sleep better now. She found a beautiful white handkerchief which a school friend had given her long ago. It had lace edging and looked almost new. I told her how pretty it was, and you know what?"

"She probably gave it to you," Mervin guessed.

"Yes, she did," confirmed Rachel. "She thinks it's too fancy for her. I don't believe I'll ever use it either, but it will be special because it's from Grandma."

"When are you going to tell us about the spelldown?" asked Scott. "It takes you the long way around to get there. It's a good thing Sal is not a car, or you would not even be half finished by the time we'd get to the singing."

Just then he commanded "Whoa" and reined in their horse Sal for a stop sign.

"Don't make me hurry, or I might forget how Mammi told it," Rachel said. "One night at a German spelling, only one other girl and Grandma had not missed a word. 'We were the only two left standing,' Grandma told me.

"The other girl was given the longest word in the ABC book. Grandma showed me the word. I asked her what it meant, and she didn't know. They were not supposed to ask what the words meant, only learn to spell them correctly. That seemed strange to me, but I just wanted to hear what happened next.

"Grandma's friend did not spell the word right away, and then Grandma saw her slowly looking down and opening her hand. In it was a white slip of paper; after glancing down at her note, she spelled the word. Since it was the longest word in the book, a new ABC speller was awarded as first prize.

"I told Grandma that was wrong because it was cheating. Mammi said she knew it was against the rules, but she didn't want to be a tattletale.

" 'How did you get the book?' I asked her. The spelling book she showed me was the very one she should have been given that night.

" 'I had studied hard,' Mammi told me, 'and my parents felt sure I'd take the floor and get a new book, which I needed.

" 'This girl, who I thought was my friend, came to me after we were church members and told me what she had done. She admitted that she knew I could spell *Unabhängigkeits-erklärung* (Declaration of Independence), and the floor and book were rightfully mine.'

"I thought it over and told Mammi that I was glad the girl confessed the truth to her and gave her the prize. Mammi certainly deserved the book. And I'm sure the girl felt better when she had straightened out that matter, too."

"Is that the end of the story?" asked Mary.

"Yes it is, and I'm sorry if it took me too long to tell it," answered Rachel.

They drew nearer to the Peachey homestead, where church had been held that day. Now they could see many other young folks coming from different directions.

Benches were set up in the kitchen, and two pitchers of water were placed on the table, along with some glasses. This was good for throats that felt dry after about thirty minutes of singing.

There was no song leader here such as Rachel was used to in the Mennonite church. Boys or girls selected a hymn of their choice and led out without the aid of a pitch pipe, tuning fork, or any instrumental music.

Rachel loved this experience. It involved many of the young people, and they sang lustily and from the heart.

After the singing, boys would ask girls if they might escort them home. Rachel saw a young man watching her. It made her uncomfortable. Sure enough, following Amish custom, he sent a friend to ask if he might take her home.

"Oh, no," Rachel replied quickly. "You see, I'm not Amish."

The boys were surprised. She sure looked Amish, and a nice-looking, well-behaved girl she was. They wondered what she was doing there then.

"Just visiting. I came with my cousins—Scott, Mervin, and Mary Eash."

"Well, Jakie Mast is taking Mary home," one of the boys informed her.

"Are you going to become Amish sometime?" another boy asked.

"Maybe, ach, I don't know," she replied.

Rachel wished she could not only take the floor, but hide beneath it as well. She was so flustered.

"What's wrong, almost-Amish *Meedel* (maiden)?"

teased Mervin on their way home. "Your face is all pink," he chuckled. "You're actually blushing.

"Aren't you ready for *Rumschpringe?*"

He didn't know of the struggle within Rachel's heart.

20
Moldy Pie

"What's for supper tonight?" Grandpa asked, as he came through the kitchen door.

"Ach, you men," exclaimed Grandma in mock disgust, "is that all you ever think of? Food?"

"Of course not, but with such good cooks and the delicious smell in this kitchen, I couldn't help but ask."

Grandma was pleased with his compliment. "Rachel and I have a surprise for you."

Grandpa washed up and hurried to his place at the table. Rachel filled the water glasses while Mammi brought the usual kettle of soup, pickled red beets, bread, butter, and applesauce.

"This is fine," said Dawdy, "but it isn't any different from what we generally have."

Rachel and Mammi just looked knowingly at each other.

"*Welle Danki gewwe* (let's give thanks)," Grandpa

murmured. They bowed their heads and hearts in silent prayer.

"Now don't eat too much," Grandma cautioned Dawdy. "Leave room for the surprise."

"More after this?" Grandpa asked.

"Yes," replied Rachel, "I made it and put the . . . ach, I almost told," she said, clamping her hands tightly to her mouth.

"I think it must be ice cream," guessed Dawdy.

"Not ice cream," Rachel told him. "If we eat fast, you will soon find out."

"We must not eat fast; it isn't good for a person," Mammi remarked. "And anyhow, we want time to talk while we eat."

Finally, everyone was finished.

"Rachel," Grandma said, "you may serve the surprise."

"You've been as jumpy as a Mexican jumping bean," laughed Grandpa, as Rachel made her way to the pantry.

Soon Rachel returned and set Grandpa's favorite pie on the table. It was an old-fashioned crumb or gravel pie. Brown sugar, eggs, and cream mixed with flour, sugar, and baking soda gave the filling a caramel taste. A mixture of butter, flour, and sugar made the crumb topping.

"What's the reason I get my favorite pie on a week night?" asked Grandpa, smiling happily.

"No special reason, Dawdy," said Rachel. "I just wanted to do something nice for you."

Yet Rachel knew she wanted to talk with Grandpa after supper about joining the Amish church.

She had planned this special treat in appreciation for his time and counsel.

"Well, now," teased Dawdy, "I'm not so sure I want to eat this pie. It looks moldy to me."

Rachel was shocked, until she saw that twinkle in his eyes and the grin upon his face. "Ach, Dawdy," she said, "it can't be moldy. I just baked it this afternoon. You're teasing."

"I could tell you a good story, though, about someone who thought pies like this were moldy."

"Will you?" asked Rachel.

"Oh, I'll think about it once," Dawdy bantered.

"Promise," said Rachel, as she was cutting the pie, "or I may not give you any."

"In that case, I sure will tell you, but not until after dishes are done. Give me time for my supper to settle," he chuckled.

It didn't take Rachel long to clear the table and do the dishes. By that time, as was often the case, some of her uncle Roy's children came over. When Rachel told them there was a story in the making, they asked if they could stay.

"Sure," welcomed Grandpa. "I always say there is room for one more." Grandpa and Grandma Eash were so glad their teenaged grandchildren cared to spend time with them and enjoy the fellowship of the larger family. They knew it was not like this in many other families, where teens may draw away to become independent, or relatives are not nearby.

"Let's see now, where should I begin?" asked Grandpa. "I guess the best place is to start at the beginning.

"When I was a young boy, there were a couple of rowdies in our neighborhood who seemingly couldn't behave. They were not what I would call bad boys, just mischievous.

"The young whippersnappers loved to go to the homes of large Amish families on a Saturday night and raid the basements. Where large families lived, plenty of pies, cakes, or cookies could be found. These had been prepared for Sunday.

"That's how we still do," Roy's daughter Mary volunteered. "Sometimes we bake almost all day on Saturday."

"Why didn't they just lock their basement doors?" asked Scott.

"There wasn't even any lock on our basement door in those days. We never felt it necessary.

"The boys said they were just having fun. Nevertheless, it was stealing. One Saturday night my mother thought she heard a noise in the basement. She listened a bit, but since all was quiet again, she went back to sleep.

"Next morning she went to the basement, and everything was in order. On Saturday she had baked five crumb pies. My sister Fanny had carried them to the basement and put them in the pie safe (cabinet).

"Well, we were all glad our things were not disturbed. My mother thought she just imagined hearing someone during the night.

"We found out soon enough that those boys had been at our house with full intentions of eating whatever goodies were stored there. However, they changed their minds. Do you know how we found out?"

"No, Dawdy," responded Rachel, "how did you find out?"

"Word began to circulate that Mrs. Eash had moldy pie. Five of them, mind you, stacked in her pie safe. Those boys had come there with intentions to find some food. In the glow of a match, they thought the white sugar and flour crumb topping was mold. They soon left our place."

"Served them right," Rachel commented. "It's funny, though, because they didn't know what good pies those were."

"Sometimes good things are mistaken for evil, but more often bad is accepted as good," Dawdy told them. " 'Woe unto them that call evil good, and good evil' " (Isaiah 5:20).

After Roy's young folks went home, Rachel confided, "I'd like to talk with you and Grandma. That is, if you aren't too tired."

"Ach, I'm never too tired to talk with you, Rachel. What's on your mind?" Dawdy asked.

"I've been thinking seriously about joining the Amish church. Roy's girls think I'm too young. They say I ought to wait until I'm seventeen or eighteen, at least. Scott says I should wait to make up my mind until after I've spent more time with my family at home again.

"I want to obey Christ as you and the other Amish church members do, in peace, humility, and simplicity. I want God's love to work in my life. I hope the Lord will mold me to be and do what he wants of me.

"You are wise and older, so what do you think I should do?"

"Rachel, I'm glad to hear a spiritual awakening is beginning in your life. In my opinion, Mammi and I still feel the plain and simple life is best."

"Then do you think people who are not living like that are on the wrong road?"

"Let me just explain it as my parents told me when I had questions such as you have. They told me, 'We are not to judge. There is one Judge, and one Lawgiver. However, we are not to live to please ourselves.'

"I think, Rachel, we lose many blessings by making ourselves believe that what we want is right. Some little things are neither right nor wrong of themselves; it's how we use them."

Rachel had wanted a straight yes-or-no answer from Dawdy.

"This is something you must work out with the Lord, Rachel," Grandpa added.

Grandma counseled, "Rachel, we would rather see you follow our way. Maybe you could be an influence to your parents. I know they are Christians, but we need them so in our church."

"I will see what my mom and dad say, but sometimes Susan and the boys make fun of my thoughts."

"Don't let that bother you, Rachel. You do what you know is right," said Dawdy.

21
An Apple a Day

Rachel had moved back with her parents when summer was over. One long weekend that fall, she spent with Grandma and Grandpa Eash.

"Rachel," said Mammi one day, "before winter, I want you to help make apple butter. I like to use fall apples rather than early ones. Early apples make better sauce, but not such good apple butter. We really ought to dry some for half-moon pies, too."

Rachel didn't know about such things, but she was glad to help.

"When I was growing up, we used to have a *Schnitzing* (apple-cutting frolic or bee)," continued Mammi. "Even when our children were still at home, we had *Schnitzings,* too. Sometimes the neighbor women would come the night before we actually cooked the *Lattwarick* (apple butter).

"We would wash, pare, and cut several bushels

of apples. The next day we cooked our apples, with sugar, vinegar, and spices, all day outdoors in a big copper kettle.

"The men would bring firewood to keep the fire going underneath the kettle. Women and girls would take turns stirring with a wooden paddle which had a handle longer than a broom has. This kept the sauce from sticking to the bottom of the kettle and burning.

"At the very last, just before ladling the apple butter into crocks, we children would throw a few pennies into the kettle."

"That seems like a strange thing to do," Rachel remarked. "Why would you throw pennies into apple butter?"

"It made them nice and shiny, just like a bright new penny," Grandma told her.

"Why don't you have apple *Schnitzings* anymore? I think it would be fun!"

"Dawdy and I don't need as much now, so I found a new way to do it. There is not as much work involved."

"How do you make it now?" asked Rachel.

"I just cook the apples on top of my stove until they are tender enough to put through the sieve and make sauce. Then I put the sauce in my big roaster, add the sugar, vinegar, and spices, and pop it into a 350-degree oven.

"I cook it for three hours and only need to stir it once each hour. It tastes just as good as the way we used to do it and takes less time."

"I'll wash and peel the apples for you," offered

Rachel, "if I know which pans to use."

"We aren't going to peel them," answered Mammi. "You wash them good, and I'll quarter them."

"But, Mammi, what about the seeds? We don't want them in our *Lattwarick*," protested Rachel.

"Don't worry, the sieve will take care of the seeds," Mammi assured her.

Rachel was learning something new again. After she had washed a large dishpanful of apples, she picked out a nice red apple and asked if she might eat it.

"Yes, you may have one. Then you need to do another panful, so they'll be ready when these are cooked," answered Mammi.

After doing the second panful, Rachel wondered if she might eat another apple.

"I think not," replied Grandma. "Too many make *Bauchweh* (stomachache). Sometimes if we get greedy, we pay for it."

"All right, Mammi. I just thought I'd ask. I don't want to be greedy. That apple tasted so good."

"I had a friend once who told me her brother had her believing 'an apple a day keeps the doctor away.' She was afraid of doctors because her earliest recollection of one was when she had broken her arm and had it set."

"How do they set an arm?" asked Rachel.

"They put the bone back in place by pulling hard on your arm to straighten it. The pain was most *wunderbaar* (terrible), and after that she never liked doctors.

"She decided, if what her brother said was true, that 'an apple a day keeps the doctor away,' three apples would keep three doctors from coming, and so forth."

"Does it really work?" asked Rachel. "I don't much care to go to the doctor either."

"All it really means is that apples are good for you. If you become greedy and eat too many, *Druwwel* (trouble) will be your lot."

"How many did your friend eat, and what happened?" asked Rachel.

"I don't know how many she ate, but she did get sick."

"Grandma, that's almost like when you wanted too much pineapple," remarked Rachel. "You really weren't greedy, just hungry for pineapple." She could not imagine her grandmother being greedy.

"But, Rachel, I didn't use self-control," admitted Mammi. "That's something I still need to battle with."

"I have a battle, too, Mammi," echoed Rachel. "My mind is made up, though. But maybe the hardest struggle is still to come."

"What do you mean?" asked Mammi.

"Last week I had a serious talk with my mom and dad about joining the Amish. They said I could if I knew that was right for me. Oh, Mammi, I am sure it is. The problem is, though, how would I get to church?"

"That will not be a problem," her grandma happily assured her. "Roy's young folks could stop by and pick you up. It isn't far out of their way."

"Maybe the boys wouldn't like that. They still call me Tagalong Rachel sometimes."

"My guess is they do it in fun. You know how our menfolk like to tease. I'll say something to them, Rachel, but I'm sure Scott and Mervin would be glad to take you.

"Do you know that Mary is going to begin instruction for church membership, too?"

"No, I didn't know that," returned Rachel. "That will make it nice, because I will be in a group with someone I know really well."

"I'm glad you didn't know she was joining, or perhaps some might say you went along because of her," commented Grandma.

"Oh, Mammi, I wouldn't do that. It's because I know I need to become a baptized Christian. My brother Timothy or my parents could bring me. But we felt it would not be proper to come by car, since they are *verbodde* (forbidden) in your church.

"Just think," exclaimed Rachel, "before long, I can say 'our church.' I'll belong, Mammi. I'll really belong!"

"I can't wait to tell Dawdy," responded Grandma, wiping a tear from her eyes. "He'll be pleased. We love your family, Rachel, but it's just something different when we get together. I can't exactly explain it."

"Isn't it strange how we started out making apple butter, then talked about an apple a day, and ended up with this conversation about church?" remarked Rachel.

"Most anything in life can have some lesson in

it," said Grandma. "Jesus taught with many stories of real life. He talked of a lost sheep, a coin, a farmer or sower, bread, water, and even new wine and old wineskins."

"That's another thing I've liked about spending a good part of the summer with you," Rachel shared. "You took many everyday happenings and turned them into interesting lessons. My mom does that too, but you lived in the olden days, and so many things were different back then."

"To hear you talk, it sounds as if I were ancient," laughed Grandma.

"No, you're not. I'm sorry, Mammi, I didn't mean it that way at all. It's just different."

"I know," responded Mammi. "It's about the good old days."

"Well," Rachel went on, "if the stories of almost drowning, broken bones, fingers cut off, two cows' tails tied together, and feathers in the living room are good old days, I'll be satisfied with living now."

"It's good to remember the past, Rachel, especially if we can learn from it. But we need to be grateful for each day God gives us.

"Now, when we have ladled the apple butter into jars, why don't you go tell Mary you will be joining her and the other church applicants in two weeks for instructions?"

Rachel's heart overflowed with peace and joy.

22
The Proving Time

Two buggies were now needed to take the young folks from Roy's to church. The boys didn't mind, as they no longer needed to share the family rig.

"Are you sure I'm not a bother?" Rachel asked Scott, as he and Mary came by for her that first Sunday.

"You have been a tagalong for so long that we would miss not having you," Scott reassured her.

"Don't mind him," Mary told her. "He was just as happy as the rest of our family when he found out you are joining church with us."

"But now Emma and Mervin have to come by themselves."

"Mervin certainly doesn't mind," Scott said. He wanted his own horse and buggy for a long time. Dad had plans to buy one for him anyway."

"Besides," Mary remarked, "sometimes after the singing it would cause a problem when one of the boys wanted to take a girl home."

"Oh," wondered Rachel, "do you suppose any boy will ever again ask to take me home from a singing?"

"The way I've seen several boys making sheep's eyes at you, Rachel, I'd say you needn't worry," Scott told her.

"I'm not worried," responded Rachel. "I just wondered because I wasn't really raised Amish."

Rachel found out soon enough that that was the least of her worries. Most people were glad to hear that one of James and Rebecca Miller's children desired to be Amish.

There were those, however, who felt Rachel must prove her sincerity. Had not her parents seemed sincere a number of years before when James united with them?

"How long did it last?" asked Minister Dan Yoder one church Sunday. The church leaders were in their *Opprote* (separate council) while the congregation was singing.

"Not even until they were married," Deacon Peter Kline answered.

"Let us remember it was not this girl's fault," mediated Bishop Yost Kramer. "I suggest we take her for instruction along with the other young folks. But she must prove herself before we take her in as one of us."

Bishop Kramer reminded them that Rachel had received good teaching from her Eash grandparents, with whom she had spent most of the summer. After that the other ministers reluctantly agreed to give her a chance to show her obedience to the *Ordnung* (lifestyle order) of the church.

James and Rebecca were well liked in the community, and many of the Amish wished they would "come back," as they put it. It was unusual for an ex-Amish family to return, but it had been known to happen. And James Miller's family was never as "worldly," according to Amish standards, as some who left their number.

Rachel still had some friction with her sister and brothers, who could not understand her decision.

"Some of my friends have been talking to me about why you are going Amish," Susie said one Sunday morning. "They think it's awful strange."

"I don't know what's so strange about it. Are you ashamed of me?"

"Of course I'm not ashamed. I just don't know what to say," Susie answered.

"Tell them I have nothing against them, my parents, or the church, but this is how I was led."

The first Sunday when Rachel joined the four girls and two boys for instruction class, she sensed she was singled out. Every eye was upon her and each remark the ministers made seemed directed specifically at Rachel Miller.

Much was said about people who stated their desire to unite with the church and later proved to have been insincere. She felt this referred to her parents, yet she hoped not.

In her heart Rachel knew she was sincere. God is everywhere, and could she not serve the Lord here as well as in the church she had attended?

Rachel soon found she was watched wherever she went. Once it was brought to her attention that she had been seen in town with her sleeves rolled above her elbows. That was too immodest. One Sunday she was told she needed to polish the gold-colored eyelets of her shoes with black polish.

It was a concern of the church that she was so young, nearly seventeen by baptism time, and that she rode in her parents' car. Rachel asked her dad to buy her a bicycle so she would use that for transportation.

"Sure," agreed James, "I'll even get one with a carrier on the front."

"Thank you, Dad. I'm glad you are so under-standing. Timothy and Susan sometimes make *Schpott* (fun) of me, and that makes me feel bad."

"I'll talk to them again," said James. "You see, Rachel, I understand, for once I was Amish and still would be had I not felt the call to go into the mission field."

"Why don't you come back again, Dad?" his daughter asked.

"Perhaps some day we will. Your mother and I have talked about it. We need to be where the Lord can best use us for his glory," James commented.

"I know, Dad," responded Rachel. "That's how I feel, too, and I want to be in God's will."

Rachel had just washed her hair one Saturday evening, but decided to leave it unpinned until Sunday morning. She took the hairpins out at night anyway. It was much more comfortable to sleep with it down.

She saw a buggy come down the driveway. Who could be coming at this hour? Thinking it was someone to see her dad, she paid no more attention. The door opened and into the kitchen came Bishop Yost Kramer and Deacon Peter Kline.

"Hello," said Rachel politely, "Come on in." James came from the living room and greeted both men.

They spoke of the weather and a few other trivial things. Then the bishop stated, "James, we would like to speak with Rachel alone."

"Sure," agreed James, "you can go on into the living room. Rebecca and I will find something to do outside. Our other young folks have left for the evening."

So it was that Rachel found herself alone with the church leaders, wondering why they had come. She noticed the stern look on Peter Kline's face.

"Rachel," he began, "we appreciate your nice long hair, but it is our belief that you should wear it pinned up and covered at all times."

"Yes, I know," Rachel answered. "But, you see, I just washed it."

"It doesn't look wet," remarked the deacon.

"No, it isn't, and I will put my hair up before I come to church."

"I would hope," said Bishop Yost, "that you do not have a habit of wearing it down around your face and hanging over your shoulders all day."

"No, I have it put up and wear my covering regularly," Rachel informed them.

"We just want to make sure you are really honest

about becoming one of us, Rachel," explained the bishop once more. "You need to prove that to us."

"What more can I do than I have done?" she asked.

"We heard you were at the singing the other Sunday evening and didn't have your covering strings tied," Deacon Peter responded.

"I didn't know I was supposed to all the time. But if that's a requirement, I will do it. I don't want to cause any trouble or be disobedient."

"Rachel," the bishop spoke again, "maybe you think we are picking on you or coming down too hard, but I have to bring a good report to the church in order to get a united vote to take you in. I hope you understand why you have to prove to us that you will cooperate."

"I will prove it," declared Rachel. "Your way is best for me, and I shall be faithful."

"Then we shall be on our way, and I'm glad we can bring a good report back to the congregation," concluded Bishop Yost, with a smile.

Peter Kline looked a little less stern as they climbed into the buggy and left.

Rachel felt humbled, yet grateful that they cared so much for her spiritual welfare.

23
Going Steady

Rachel had been attending Sunday evening singings regularly. She enjoyed them immensely. More often than not, she would go with either Scott and Mary, or Mervin and Emma, but return home with someone else.

Rachel was a lovely girl, and even though she dressed plainly, strictly in the *Ordnung* (regulations) of the church, she was attractive. Norman Kuhns had taken Rachel home from singings more than any other boy.

One night he asked her, "Rachel, would it be all right if I come and take you to the singing two weeks from tonight?"

"Well, I guess, if you really want to," she answered.

"Of course I do, or I wouldn't have asked."

"Then it's settled," Rachel replied. After a few days she told Scott that he and Mary needn't stop by for her.

"Oh, are we are losing our Tagalong Rachel?" he teased.

Rachel just laughed and made a face at him.

"Who is it? Norman K.?" asked Scott.

"Wouldn't you like to know?" bantered Rachel.

"I'll know soon enough. We always watch who the girls leave with."

Rachel was back home with her own parents for the winter. She did miss Mammi and Dawdy, but it was good to be with her family again.

Her brothers and Susan were nicer to her since their father had talked with them. When any of her Amish friends came to visit, they accepted them politely.

Susan had been keeping company with a nice young man for several years and was engaged to be married in the spring. Rachel's cousin Emma was making plans, only it was supposed to be a secret.

After a dozen times of escorting Rachel to and from the singing, Norman asked her to go steady.

"I don't know, Norman. May I think about it?"

"Sure," answered Norman. "But I hope the answer will be yes."

"Are you sure it will be all right with your parents? I think it's real important that parents' approve of the company we keep."

"I agree with you, but I can tell you right now my folks think highly of you."

"Mine like you, too," Rachel said.

"Then I see no problem," declared Norman.

"Just the same, give me a little time."

"I will, Rachel, but is it okay if I say something

to my folks about it, too? Just so I can tell you how pleased they are," he said, chuckling.

So that's how they parted, with Rachel's consent to go with him in two weeks again.

Norman had some exciting news when he came for Rachel on Sunday night. "Rachel," he told her almost as soon as they left for the singing, "I've got good news."

"What is it, Norman?" she questioned.

"Some of our friends are planning a day at the zoo next Saturday and asked if we would like to go, too."

"That sounds like fun. Are any other couples going?"

"Sure, several of them," replied Norman, his heart beating a bit faster. "You said 'other couples,' Rachel. That means, then, that you consider us as going steady."

Rachel blushed a deep pink. What had she said?

"I didn't mean to be forward. It wasn't meant that way."

"How was it meant?" asked Norman.

"Well, I only wanted to know if other girls would be there. I didn't want to be the only girl, you know."

It was a lame explanation, but it was the best she could do under the circumstances. She lifted her hand to shield her face for a moment.

Norman grinned and assured her, "Of course there will be other girls going. But I'd like to have my answer to the question of two weeks ago. Will we be going steady?"

"Yes, Norman, my parents said they agree to that if I'm sure it's right for me."

"And is it right for you?"

"Like Dawdy used to say," said Rachel, giggling a bit, "it's as right as rain."

Norman felt ten feet tall. This lovely girl was his special friend now, and no one else would be taking her for buggy rides to social gatherings any more. He knew that once word got around they were keeping company regularly, others would not try to break up the friendship. It just wasn't done.

"Tell me who the others are that will be going to the zoo," coaxed Rachel.

"Maybe I will have you wait and be surprised," Norman responded, with a twinkle in his eyes.

"You wouldn't!" protested Rachel. "Men sure like to tease. Don't keep me in suspense, or I just might change my mind about going steady!" She could play little tricks, too.

Now it was Norman's turn to say "You wouldn't!" He decided to tell her, and they began to plan the day.

"Can we drive it with the buggy?" asked Rachel.

"We can if we start early. All of us have fast-paced horses, so we should have time to see all there is to see."

"What about food? Where will we eat?"

"Now that's where you girls come in handy," Norman laughed. "Bring well-filled picnic baskets, and we boys will spread blankets along the river and help get rid of the food."

It sounded like so much fun. Rachel thought it

would be a good way to become better acquainted with a few of the girls she didn't know well. She had gone to the zoo a few times with her parents and once with both grandparents, but this was special.

When Rachel told her sister that she had an *Alder* (steady boyfriend), Susan said warmly, "I'm glad you are going to the zoo with an Amish *Bu* (boy)."

Rachel thought for one moment she detected a wistful look in Susan's eyes. Was she wishing she could go to the zoo with them in those buggy rides? Could she accept it that her sister now had an Amish boyfriend?

Rachel wondered if she herself had changed and no longer took her brothers' and sister's remarks to heart or let them hurt her.

The anxiously awaited day had come. Rachel stood on the front porch with her basket of goodies by her feet. She had combed her hair neatly and tied her covering strings properly. The dress she chose to wear was blue, a favorite color.

James looked out the door, and it seemed as if he had suddenly gone back in time. Rachel looked exactly as his beloved Rebecca looked when she was almost eighteen. His thoughts were interrupted by the sound of a horse and buggy stirring up the gravel in his driveway.

"My," James called to his daughter, "you had better tell Norman to watch out for the cops. I think he almost broke the speed limit coming down my drive."

"Oh, you!" exclaimed Rachel, smiling fondly. Rebecca appeared at the doorway to say hello to Norman and wish them a good day.

A good day they had, too. The weather was beautiful, and oh, so much to see at the zoo. At noon the boys spread out their blankets in a shady spot by a stream, and the girls brought their food baskets.

They bowed their heads in silent prayer. Then the girls set out their creations, and it seemed that each had tried to outdo the others.

"I'm so full," said Jonas Mast, "I think I'll just sit here and rest awhile before going back to see more animals."

"Not a bad idea," agreed Levi Chupp. They sat and talked of many things.

"We sound almost like my relatives when they get together," commented Rachel. "They talk of bygone days and how hard it was back then.

"Once they remembered how one child caught her arm in the washing machine wringer. Two weeks later, another one had several fingers cut off in a farm accident, and a month later, the baby broke her arm. This was all in the same family, yet they called it the good old days."

"We know just what you mean," laughed the others. "We've heard it many times, too."

"But I always enjoy hearing them tell of their growing-up years. We have good parents," said Ruth Hershberger.

"And Dawdies too," remarked Rachel.

"You learned much from them, didn't you, Rachel?" asked Fern Mullet.

"Yes, I certainly did," she replied, in a soft, intense tone.

"But now we are going steady," stated Norman, "so Dawdies will have to share."

And Rachel's face glowed as she gave him a happy look.

24
Crossed Over

Baptismal Sunday finally arrived. The day before, Rachel and all those who were to be taken into the church had met for final instructions with the congregational leaders. They were the bishop, two other ministers, and the deacon, whose duties included visiting the sick and collecting alms money.

The leaders were especially solemn at that meeting, for it was an important step which these young people were about to take. Had they been thoroughly admonished?

When everyone was seated in the living room of the bishop's home where they had gathered, Deacon Peter Kline read a passage of Scripture. Then one of the ministers prayed from the prayer book as they reverently knelt.

After they were seated again, Bishop Yost Kramer cleared his throat and began to speak earnestly. "It is important that we have this meeting with you today. Proverbs eleven, verse fourteen, says: 'Where no counsel is, the people fall; but in the multitude of counsellors there is safety.'

"Therefore, we want to be sure you understand fully that the vows you will make tomorrow are serious and not to be broken. They are made before God and his people."

Rachel had returned home with these words firmly fixed in her mind. They were still vividly fresh the next morning as she filed into the room and took her place near the ministers, among the rest of those receiving baptism.

Her parents and two brothers and sister were present to witness the sealing of her vows. Both sets of grandparents were also able to attend. It was a special day in all of their lives.

A holy quietness seemed to fall upon the people as the first minister stood up to speak. His message was simple and direct, from a farmer who had given himself to daily Bible study, prayer, and the leading of the Holy Spirit.

Rachel knew that Amish leaders did not attend seminaries to take training as ministers nor accept money for their services. The Lord called them, and he would surely provide for their sustenance and spiritual food for the congregation, she believed.

Minister Dan Yoder spoke first this Sunday morning. He began preaching from the book of Genesis, and about God's purposes. "How long," he asked, "was it from the time of creation until the fall of man? Not very long. God had prepared such a nice world and he called it good.

"But sin soon entered and spoiled it all. You young people who are before us here, take heed. God has begun a new life within you, and Satan stands ready, yes, even eager, to spoil it. Don't let it happen.

"Be faithful to the teaching you have been given these last months. Live for the Lord and not to please yourselves, and you won't go wrong."

Rachel listened intently. She observed her father nodding his head in agreement. Others noticed, too, and wondered why he hadn't stayed as one with them.

Norman was sitting where he had a good view of the baptismal group. He hardly saw any of them except Rachel. She looked so pure and innocent. She was the youngest of the seven seated there.

How he wished she were older, closer to marrying age, but he would be willing to wait. He must not think of that now. With determination, he brought his thoughts back to the message.

It was still early in the service, but a baby began to cry, and one of Lewis Lehman's twins threw a temper tantrum. Mrs. Lehman took her screaming child to the washhouse for a good *Bletsching* (paddling). Rachel tried not to let these disturbances interfere with her worship.

After Scripture reading and prayer, the bishop began to preach. He, too, spoke out of a heart filled with concern for the young souls present there. "We appreciate the way you have conformed to the rules and regulations according to our belief for the church," he affirmed them kindly.

"Many temptations shall befall you, but I advise, yes, admonish you, be faithful to that which you promise here on bended knee today. Do not gratify your own selfish desires, but consider others better than yourself. Love the brotherhood. Serve God, and keep his commandments."

Rachel was so glad her parents had not quit speaking the Amish language. It made it easier for her to understand the German, and she had been grasping more of it as she attended Amish services. But it was not so easy for Susan and her brothers because English was used in their Mennonite congregation.

Susan began to get a bit restless and wondered why time seemed to drag. Her mother, on the other hand, was thrilled to hear once more the familiar passages she had heard many times as a young child.

James noticed the rapt expression on his wife's face. Perhaps he should offer to join with Rebecca's people. But if he would, he wanted it to be for good this time.

James also realized that his two sons and Susan would object. Yet he felt they could serve God faithfully in either a Mennonite or an Amish church. Both had good Bible preaching and a commitment to fear and obey God and express God's love in daily life.

James understood, however, that many did not share this outlook. He thought of Jesus' words concerning salvation: "Thou shalt love the Lord thy God with all thy heart, and with all thy soul, and with all thy mind. Thou shalt love thy neighbour as thyself. On these two commandments hang all the law and the prophets" (from Matthew 22:37-40).

It was now time for the applicants to kneel facing forward to receive water baptism. The deacon arose to assist. He had a pitcher of water in his hand and waited as the bishop asked each youth questions. They each answered to give witness to their faith.

"Are you willing, by the help and grace of God, to *renounce* the world, the devil, your own flesh and blood, and be *obedient* only to God and his church? (Yes.)

"Are you willing to walk with Christ and his church and to remain faithful through life and until death? (Yes.)

"Can you confess that Jesus Christ is the Son of God? (I confess that Jesus Christ is the Son of God.)"

Then after a prayer, the bishop cupped his hands upon each head and said, "I baptize you in the name of the Father, and of the Son, and of the Holy Ghost." At the mention of each name, the deacon poured into the bishop's hands a little water, which dripped over the youth's head.

Generally the bishop's wife also assisted by removing each girl's head covering so it wouldn't get wet and extending to her the right hand of fellowship and the holy kiss. Today the bishop's wife was absent because of illness. It was therefore proper and acceptable for another minister's wife or an older sister in full fellowship to perform this duty.

When Bishop Yost asked that one of the sisters

come forward, there was no immediate response. Eva Gingerich, who was sitting next to Grandma Ellie, nudged her and whispered, "I think you should be the one, Ellie."

With that encouragement, Ellie rose to her feet, made her way to the end of the bench, and at the proper time removed each prayer cap. How thrilled Rachel was to see dear Mammi have a part in her special day.

When the vows had been spoken, baptism administered, and each girl's prayer cap replaced on her head, the bishop took Rachel by the hand and bade her rise. As she stood up, he said, "May the Lord God complete the good work which he has begun in you and strengthen and comfort you to a blessed end through Jesus Christ. Amen."

Pronouncing her a full-fledged member, he presented her to Grandma Ellie for the welcoming kiss and embrace. Tears of joy mingled as Ellie welcomed her granddaughter, and the handclasp was firm. Ellie likewise greeted the other young women just baptized. The bishop welcomed the young men similarly and wished them peace.

After the service and a little visiting, Rachel's parents were about to leave before the noon fellowship meal. They knew that members might feel bound to shun them by not eating in a circle with them, since they had left membership in the Amish church. James wanted to avoid any awkward scene.

Before they left, Mammi said, "Rebecca, Dawdy and I want your family and James' parents to come over this evening for a light supper and some singing. This is a day that has made me very happy, and I want it to end that way."

"I'll see what James says," Rebecca told her.

"We do have services at our church tonight," James replied, "but we can worship in song at your place, too. Yes, Rebecca, if you want to go, we will."

Norman was invited, too, and so was Roy's family. After a meal of sandwiches, potato salad, pie, and mixed fruit, the family was ready to sing.

"First, though," interrupted Mammi. "Rachel, I have something for you."

She went to the bedroom and returned with a brown package. "Use it always," Grandma urged.

Rachel opened it and was delighted to see it was a German Bible. "Thank you, Mammi. I will read it often."

"Well," teased Scott, "I suppose we can't call you Tagalong Rachel anymore, now that you and Norman are steadies. He'll have you following him all the time, and soon we'll call you Norman-Rachel."

"Oh, stop it," returned Rachel, pretending to box his ears.

"Rachel, now that you became a member of the body of believers today, would you like to choose the first song?" asked Dawdy.

She chose her and Dawdy's favorite German song, "Gott ist die Liebe (God is love)."

God loved her enough to draw her to himself. He brought her through the troubled waters of decision. She had made her choice and crossed over.

What a deep, settled peace was hers! She was sure-enough Amish.

The Author

Mary Christner Borntrager realized at an early age the importance of reading. Her love of good books and her heritage from Amish life prompted her to write two previous novels, *Ellie* and *Rebecca*.

Mary was one of ten children in an Amish home. Many of the happenings in this book were taken from her own growing-up years.

Her early education was eight grades of public school. Later she attended teacher-training institute at Eastern Mennonite College, Harrisonburg, Virginia. For seven years she taught at a Christian day school.

After her children were grown, Mary acquired a certificate in childcare and youth social work from the University of Wisconsin. For twelve years she and her late husband, John, worked with emotionally disturbed youth.

Mary is a member of the Ohioana Library Association of Columbus and does public speaking. She is a member of the Hartville (Ohio) Mennonite Church, where she is a substitute teacher for an adult Sunday school class and serves on the hospitality committee.

She finds her four children and eleven grandchildren a great comfort and joy. Her hobbies include reading, quilting, embroidery work, writing, and Bible memory.

Mary desires that this book may bring other parents, grandparents, and children to closer relationships with each other. "We can learn so much, and we have much to share," she says.